D0045604

The Secret of the Golden Pavilion

BY CAROLYN KEENE

GROSSET & DUNLAP
Publishers • New York
A member of The Putnam & Grosset Group

PRINTED ON RECYCLED PAPER

Contents

CHAPTER		PAGE
I	A MOONLIGHT BURGLAR	1
II	A SUSPECT	8
III	STRANGE SYMBOLS	18
IV	A REWARDING CHASE	27
V	DOUBLE WORRIES	34
VI	A DISASTROUS DANCE	40
VII	A STUDIO ACCIDENT	49
VIII	THE SURPRISING CLUE	58
IX	THE GOLDEN PAVILION	67
X	A DAYTIME GHOST	77
XI	A TANTALIZING GIFT	85
XII	THE LEI MAKER'S HINT	92
XIII	A VALUABLE DISCOVERY	100
XIV	MEETING A SHARK	108
XV	THE SILVERSWORD'S SECRET	119
XVI	THE SPECTER	127
XVII	VOLCANO BIRDS	138
XVIII	AN EXPLOSION	147
XIX	A KING'S TREASURE	157
XX	ALOHA!	170

Nancy and Ned tried to escape, but it was too late

CHAPTER I

A Moonlight Burglar

NANCY DREW, her lovely blue eyes sparkling with excitement, stared in fascination from the cabin of a private helicopter. The craft was headed for the River Heights airport, a few miles beyond. Below, the rooftops of the town stood out clearly in the moonlight.

"We're almost home, Togo," Nancy said to the terrier beside her. Fastened to his collar was a blue ribbon that he had won at a dog show in a city some distance away.

Leaning forward, Nancy asked the pilot, "Could we please go lower? I'd love to see my house from the air."

The young man shook his head. "It's against regulations. Maybe these will help you." He handed her a pair of binoculars.

Nancy adjusted them and in a moment her home came into focus. "I see it!" she exclaimed.

But a second later she suddenly gasped in alarm, "A man's climbing into a dormer window on our third floor!"

"You mean a burglar?" the pilot asked.

"Yes. All our windows on the first and second floors are wired for a burglar alarm. The thief must know that. Oh, dear, he may harm Hannah!"

Quickly Nancy explained that Hannah Gruen was the Drews' housekeeper and that Mrs. Gruen had been like a mother to her since she was a little girl and had lost her own mother.

"Radio the airport tower, please!" Nancy urged. "Tell them what's happening and ask them to page my father. He's waiting for me. He can contact the police to catch that burglar!"

Instantly the pilot made the call. Then, at Nancy's request, he began to circle above the Drew home. Less than five minutes later, they saw the burglar step out backward from the dormer window onto a long, slender ladder. In his hand was a brief case.

"It must be one of Dad's," Nancy told the pilot.

The intruder made a nimble descent. Then he collapsed the ladder into a small bundle, picked it up, and disappeared among the trees that lined the Drew driveway.

"Please relay all this to the tower," Nancy begged.

The pilot followed her request, then said, "I'd better get to the field pronto."

His landing was cleared and soon the helicopter was standing on the concrete runway. Nancy tucked Togo under one arm and her purse under the other, while the pilot grabbed her week-end bag. Then the two hurried to the gate.

At the exit stood a taxi driver whom Nancy knew well. "Good evening, Joe," she said.

" 'Evening," he replied. "Your father asked me to drive you home. I hear you've been having some excitement at your house. Mr. Drew said something about his fetching the police and nabbing a burglar."

"Then Dad did get the message!" Nancy exclaimed. "Let's hope they caught the thief before he got off the grounds."

She thanked the pilot for his assistance, then ran to Joe's taxi and hopped in. He drove as quickly as possible to Nancy's home.

As the taxi came to a halt at the front door of the large, brick house, Mr. Drew stepped from the doorway and took Nancy in his arms. "So good to see you again," said the tall, distinguished-looking lawyer.

"It's good to be here," his daughter replied. "The burglar— Did you catch him?"

"Unfortunately, no."

Togo, who had scampered into the house, was running around in circles and yipping with joy at being home. In a moment Hannah Gruen appeared from the rear of the house.

"Are you all right, Hannah?" Nancy asked, as she hugged the housekeeper affectionately.

"Oh, yes. But to tell the truth, I'm mighty embarrassed. I didn't even hear that burglar," she went on. "I dropped off to sleep waiting for you and your father, and never woke up once. By the way, what did the man take?" she asked Mr. Drew.

The lawyer said that so far as he could find out, the burglar had been after only one thing—a brief case containing papers relating to a new case which he had just taken.

"The intruder may have wanted these for some special reason, but also he may have been after an odd-looking object that was in the brief case. My client was sending it to you, Nancy. It was a copy of a rare old Polynesian artifact—a wooden figure, half human and half bird. It had little monetary value, so I'm puzzled about that aspect of the burglary."

"Perhaps," said Nancy, "the thief believed the piece to be old and rare."

"Possibly," her father agreed.

Nancy inquired how the burglar might have learned about the contents of the brief case. Mr. Drew stared into space a moment, then answered, "I had luncheon today with my new client, Mr. Sakamaki. He's a Hawaiian. He talked rather freely about his case. It was a public restaurant and perhaps the burglar was seated nearby listening to the conversation."

"Does the case involve something Polynesian?" Nancy asked.

"Well, yes and no," the lawyer replied. "I'd prefer that Mr. Sakamaki tell you the whole story himself. You may pick up a few points which I missed," he complimented his daughter. "When I happened to mention to him that you loved to solve mysteries, he was interested at once."

Mr. Drew looked directly at Nancy, a slight smile playing around the corners of his mouth. "There is a very unusual mystery in connection with the case. Mr. Sakamaki would like you to solve it for him."

Nancy's face broke into a broad grin. "And I'd like to do it!" she said eagerly. "How soon may I talk to Mr. Sakamaki?"

"Tomorrow morning at my office."

While Hannah prepared a midnight snack of angel cake and fruit juice, Mr. Drew went to the telephone and called police headquarters. The sergeant on duty reported that his squad had not apprehended the burglar as yet. The clue of the collapsible ladder was an excellent one, he said, and his men had stopped and searched a hundred cars in the general area of the Drew home. But no ladder had been found in any of the automobiles.

"We'll keep on looking," the sergeant promised. "Something may turn up yet."

The next morning after breakfast Nancy and her father set out for his office. It was not long after they arrived that Mr. Drew's secretary announced a caller.

"Mr. Kamuela Sakamaki is here."

"Please show him in," Mr. Drew replied.

A smiling man about forty years old walked in. He was of medium height, with lightly bronzed skin and friendly dark eyes. Mr. Drew presented him to Nancy.

"I'm very happy to meet you," Mr. Sakamaki said. "And I hope that you, as well as your father, will consent to taking my case."

As everyone sat down, the caller explained that he was part Polynesian, part Japanese. "My Polynesian first name means 'Sam' and when necessary I use the English version for business. I am very proud of my Polynesian forebears."

Mr. Sakamaki explained that he had perfected certain methods for finishing handmade furniture —an art practiced by his Polynesian ancestors. Like them, he used sharkskin instead of sandpaper.

"At present I am lecturing and demonstrating in a furniture factory here. Mrs. Sakamaki and I have rented a house in River Heights for a year."

He went on to say that he had recently inherited a large estate of both money and property from his grandfather, Nikkio Sakamaki, in Honolulu. The estate was called Kaluakua. Abruptly he asked:

"Miss Drew, would you like to go out there to solve my mystery?" From his pocket he brought out a paper on which two symbols had been drawn. "I believe these are a clue that will help."

He handed the paper to Nancy, who studied the strange figures. "Do you know what they mean?" she asked.

"No, I'm ashamed to say I don't," Mr. Sakamaki replied. "I intended trying to find out but haven't had a chance."

The Hawaiian said that shortly before his grandfather's death, the elderly man had mailed the symbols to him without any translation. But a letter accompanying the strange piece of paper had said:

"Never sell or give away Kaluakua until you solve its mystery."

CHAPTER II

A Suspect

As Nancy stared at the strange symbols, her heart beat a little faster. This was a new and different kind of mystery for her to solve!

"It sounds like a fascinating case," she commented. Nancy recalled the exciting adventures she had had solving *The Secret of the Old Clock,* her first mystery, and how many thrilling moments she had experienced during her recent adventure, *The Haunted Showboat*. But none of the mysteries had started out with a more challenging clue than the one just presented to her.

Mr. Sakamaki smiled. "You will love Kaluakua. The estate is right along the water of the Waikiki Beach area of Honolulu. It has beautiful gardens and a lovely house, and is a perfect place for a vacation."

Nancy looked toward her father. She wondered what he was thinking.

8

The lawyer smiled and said, "Mr. Sakamaki, I should think you would want to go there yourself and attend to matters."

"I suppose I should," the Hawaiian replied, "but it would be most inconvenient at this time. Many pressing business matters will keep me on the mainland." He turned to Nancy. "We Hawaiians call the people in the Continental United States 'mainlanders.' "

Mr. Sakamaki now amazed the Drews by saying that actually there were two mysteries in connection with settling his grandfather's estate. Only that day he had learned of two claimants, a brother and a sister, who had suddenly appeared in Honolulu, declaring that they were grandchildren of the deceased man.

"Besides that disturbing news," Mr. Sakamaki went on, "I have had word from the caretaker that there have been queer happenings at Kaluakaa."

"What kind of happenings?" Nancy asked.

"For one thing," the caller replied, "a stranger was seen lurking on the estate beach, and when the caretaker went to question him, the man took off hurriedly in a boat. Then, there is a Golden Pavilion on the grounds, and someone has been hacking the floor of it."

"A Golden Pavilion?" Nancy repeated.

Mr. Sakamaki said that it was a circular open building about thirty feet in diameter. It had columns and a roof, all covered with gold leaf.

"It sounds very unusual," Nancy remarked. "Is the secret of Kaluakua connected with this pavilion?"

Mr. Sakamaki shrugged. "Wherever or whatever the secret is, I should like to have it discovered as quickly as possible. I intend to present the estate to Honolulu, with the Golden Pavilion to be used as an outdoor theater. You see, I really don't need Kaluakua for myself financially. And I have a lovely home in Honolulu where I prefer living."

Then the man's face clouded as he continued, "I keep forgetting about the Chatleys. They are the claimants. If they should prove their case, I suppose the estate would have to be split three ways. It is doubtful if they would agree to donate Kaluakua to Honolulu. They probably would want to sell it and take the money to the mainland."

Mr. Drew now spoke up. "You never heard about these relatives from your grandfather or anyone else?"

Mr. Sakamaki shook his head. "These people are claiming that my grandfather had a wife in California some years before he moved to Honolulu. They further claim that my grandfather abandoned his wife and a baby daughter. Knowing my grandfather as I did, I cannot imagine him doing such a thing. He was somewhat eccentric, but full of kindness. My own parents, who are deceased, never mentioned any such thing taking place."

"Was your grandfather a Hawaiian?"

"No, he came from Japan. But he married a Polynesian."

Mr. Sakamaki told the Drews that the claimants' full names were Roy Chatley and his married sister, Janet Chatley Lee. Both were about forty-five years of age.

"As I said, I have never seen them nor heard of them before," Mr. Sakamaki continued. "I had come to your father, Nancy, to ask him to help me settle the estate before this complication arose. I just received a letter about the Chatleys from the bank in Honolulu which is acting as executor. Now I've come to beg you, Mr. Drew, to investigate this new angle."

"Just how did your grandfather's will read regarding beneficiaries?"

"It stated simply that everything was left to any living grandchildren," Mr. Sakamaki replied. "I thought I was the only living blood relative until the Chatleys suddenly came into the picture."

He went on to say that Mr. Drew would be handling the legal angles pertaining to the settling of the estate, including the Chatleys' claim. He had thought Nancy would like to take over the part of his case having to do with the secret at Kaluakua.

"Oh, I'd love to," said Nancy eagerly. "May I, Dad?"

The lawyer smiled fondly at his daughter. "There is only one hitch," he said. "I cannot leave here immediately. Besides, I think my first stop should be Los Angeles, where I'll look into the background of these claimants to the estate. Valuable time would be lost before I could reach Honolulu."

Mr. Sakamaki leaned forward in his chair. "Perhaps," he said to Nancy, "you have some young friends who would go with you? And also your housekeeper?"

Nancy did not reply at once. Her mind flew to her two chums, Bess Marvin and Bess's tomboy cousin George Fayne, but she knew that the expense involved in such a trip would be prohibitive.

The Hawaiian apparently had guessed her thoughts. Smiling, he said, "I want this mystery solved. Expense means nothing to me. I'll finance the trip for the entire group."

Nancy was overwhelmed by the offer. Feeling that it was up to her father to make the decision, she waited for him to speak.

Mr. Drew gazed out his office window a few moments before replying. Then he turned to Mr. Sakamaki. "I will consent to all of this on one condition. The expense involved will be my fee."

"As you wish," Mr. Sakamaki said. "I will do

everything I can to make it a most enjoyable stay for you." He arose and shook hands with the two Drews. "You have made me very happy," he added, "and I will leave you now to make your own plans. I will be in touch with you soon."

Bowing slightly, he left the office. At once Nancy went over to her father and threw her arms about his neck. "It sounds marvelous, doesn't it? Almost like a dream. I can hardly believe it!"

Her father agreed, and said he hoped that Bess and George would be able to go with Nancy, as well as Hannah Gruen. "I'll make arrangements for you all to fly to Honolulu as soon as you let me know if the girls can go."

He suddenly noticed that his daughter's smile had faded. Her expression was tense and she was staring out the window.

"What's the matter?" the lawyer asked her.

Nancy pointed and her father turned to look in that direction. On the rooftop of a nearby office building a man was opening a collapsible ladder. As the Drews watched, he placed it against a window of the adjoining building.

"He may be the thief who got into our house last night!" Nancy cried out. "It looks like the same kind of ladder!"

Instantly Mr. Drew turned to his telephone. He put in a call to a lawyer he knew who occupied the office where the open window was. After a few moments of conversation, he hung up and said to Nancy, "The man is a window washer, but we probably should investigate him."

"Let's go talk to him right now," Nancy urged.

Mr. Drew agreed and they went immediately to the office of his lawyer friend. They learned from him that the window washer's name was Abe Antok and that he worked for the Acme Window Cleaning Company.

Nancy hastened to the window where the man was working. After a few casual remarks to Abe Antok, she asked, "Isn't it unusual for ladders to be used for washing office windows?"

"Yes, ma'am, it is," Abe replied. "But my boss and me, we been inventin' this ladder. You notice it's kind of special. We hope to put it on the market someday and make a lot of money. But a few kinks have to be ironed out yet. I use it in places that are hard to get to."

"I see," said Nancy. "By the way, how high will it reach?"

"Oh, very high, miss," Abe replied proudly.

"Could it reach to the third floor of a house?"

"Oh, sure," Abe answered. "I've used it a couple of times for that. Worked fine."

During the conversation Nancy had made up her mind that Abe in no way seemed like a housebreaker. A new thought suddenly came to her and she asked, "Do you ever rent out this kind of ladder?"

"He may be the thief!" Nancy cried out

Abe Antok looked at Nancy in amazement. "That's a funny question, miss," he said. "As a matter of fact, I did, just once. That was last night."

"What did the person who rented the ladder want to do with it?" Nancy asked quickly.

"To tell you the truth, miss," Abe replied, "Mr. Jim O'Keefe—that's the name of the man who rented the ladder—said he wanted to try it out. He came to our place just about quittin' time and gave my boss and me a great sales talk. Said he handled stock or something like that. He told us he could set us up in business and make a lot of money for us. We fell for it and gave him the ladder to try out."

"Where is Jim O'Keefe now?" Nancy inquired eagerly.

Abe Antok's face took on a sour look. "My boss and me sure had the wool pulled over our eyes. We found the ladder back of the shop this mornin'. When we didn't hear nothin' from O'Keefe, my boss called the hotel where he was stayin'. He'd skipped out without payin' his bill!"

"That's very interesting," said Nancy. "What did this man look like?"

Abe described Jim O'Keefe as being of medium height, dark, slender, and with thinning hair.

"Did he have any outstanding characteristics by which you could identify him?" Nancy inquired.

Abe thought for a moment. Then he answered, "Yes, he did. O'Keefe drummed on my boss's desk with his fingers. Then he raised up his two forefingers and put the tips of 'em together. Kind of a funny thing to do, wasn't it?"

Nancy agreed. She thanked Abe for answering her questions, then hurried over to her father who was conversing with his lawyer friend. "I have a wonderful clue to our thief," she said excitedly, then told the two men about Jim O'Keefe.

Mr. Drew asked permission to use the phone and called the police. Captain McGinnis thanked him for the new clue and said he would get in touch with the lawyer as soon as he had any news.

Nancy and her father returned to Mr. Drew's office. For several minutes they discussed the mystery—Kaluakua and its secret, the strange claimants to the Sakamaki estate, the burglar, and the proposed trip to Honolulu.

Suddenly Nancy chuckled softly. "You know, Dad, there's one thing I haven't told you. Certain friends of Bess, George, and myself are going on a chartered plane trip from Emerson College to Honolulu when their vacation begins."

"You mean Ned Nickerson, Burt Eddleton, and Dave Evans?" her father asked.

"That's right, Dad. We'll have a whole fleet of mainland detectives to solve the Kaluakua mystery!"

CHAPTER III

Strange Symbols

MR. DREW'S eyes were twinkling. "This sounds like a Hawaiian house party," he remarked. "Seriously, I'm glad the boys will be there to help solve the mystery. There are a few angles to this case that worry me, and I'll feel better with a crowd of you at Kaluakua."

"I'll call Bess and George right away," said Nancy. "Suppose I make it on the outside phone, Dad. See you later."

She gave him a quick kiss and left. From his secretary's desk, Nancy called first Bess, then George. No one answered at either of their homes. Nancy, eager to share her secret and hopeful that her friends could make the trip, was disappointed.

"Oh, well, I'll try later," she said to herself.

The young sleuth decided to start work on the case immediately. First, she went to the library to see if she could learn from reference books there the meaning of the Polynesian symbols which Nikkio Sakamaki had sent to his grandson. The reference librarian was very helpful, but neither she nor Nancy could find the answer to the riddle.

"I'm sorry," said Miss Taylor, who knew the young detective well. "I suppose you're working on another mystery. Perhaps I can help you. Something just occurred to me. I believe I know the very person who might be able to tell you what these symbols mean. He's Professor Wharton. I understand he speaks many languages and is an authority on hieroglyphics and other forms of ancient writing."

Nancy smiled. "That's wonderful. I'd like to talk to him. Where does he live?"

"Just a minute," Miss Taylor replied. She opened a drawer of her desk and looked through a stack of cards. Presently she pulled one out. "Here it is. He lives in the newly developed section of River Heights called Elwynd Estates. I'm sorry I don't have the name of the street."

"I'll be able to find him," Nancy said, eager to start. "Thank you very much for everything, Miss Taylor."

The young sleuth hurried home to get her convertible, then drove out to Elwynd Estates. At the entrance were large stone pillars with a small office to one side. She inquired where Professor

Wharton lived and was given directions to Hilltop Road. Hoping that the elderly man would be at home, she hurried to his house, parked the car, and went up the front walk.

She lifted the huge knocker on the front door. After a moment the door was opened by a tall, frail-looking man, with brilliant blue eyes and a shock of white hair.

"Professor Wharton?" Nancy inquired.

The man nodded, and asked her to come in. As Nancy introduced herself and told why she was there, Mrs. Wharton came forward and was introduced.

"I am very much interested in trying to help you," the professor said, as Nancy opened her purse and handed him the piece of paper bearing the symbols which Mr. Sakamaki had given her. "Ah, yes," the professor murmured.

Mrs. Wharton asked Nancy to be seated, and her husband excused himself to go to his study. He was gone only a few moments.

"I have your answer," he said, smiling. "These are ancient Polynesian symbols, to be sure. The first one means *water,* and the second *sleep* or *death*."

"Water, and sleep or death," Nancy repeated thoughtfully. "This is a wonderful help to me. Thank you very, very much, Professor Wharton."

Nancy was so excited by what she had learned that she decided to stop at her father's office and tell him about the meaning of the symbols. To her delight, Mr. Sakamaki was there.

Mr. Drew looked at his daughter intently, then broke into a chuckle. "Mr. Sakamaki, I can tell you right now that Nancy has already solved one part of our mystery."

"So soon?" the Islander asked unbelievingly.

Nancy told the two men how she had learned the meaning of the Polynesian symbols. "Have you any idea, Mr. Sakamaki, what your grandfather could have meant by water and sleep or death?" she asked.

Mr. Sakamaki shook his head. "I can only make a guess. Since Grandfather told me not to sell Kaluakua before I learned its mystery, I would say that perhaps he meant the Golden Pavilion contains the secret because it is near the water. As to the sleep or death symbol, I have no idea."

"Is it possible," Nancy asked, "that someone who was dear to your grandfather sleeps in death beneath the pavilion?"

After a few moments of thoughtful silence, Mr. Sakamaki said that he was sure such was not the case. Then he changed the subject of conversation.

"I came here to tell your father that I have just had an airmail letter from the caretaker, Kiyabu. It said that the night before, at dusk, a mysterious native dancing girl had appeared in the pavilion. Kiyabu claimed that she looked like a ghost dancing the hula. He and his wife sneaked up on the figure with the thought of questioning her. But just before they reached the pavilion, she seemed to vanish into nothingness, and that frightened them."

"A ghost!" Nancy cried out excitedly.

"One could come to that conclusion," Mr. Sakamaki replied. "But I have a theory that some person or persons may have cleverly rigged up a contrivance to make it appear as if a ghost were dancing in the pavilion."

"But why should anyone go to all that trouble?" Nancy asked.

The Hawaiian could give no explanation. He wondered whether he might have some enemies who had in some way heard of Kaluakua's secret, and were trying to learn what it was. They probably figured it to be a great treasure.

"Nancy," the man said earnestly, "you may be running into plenty of *pilikia*."

"Pilikia?" Nancy questioned.

"That means trouble," Mr. Sakamaki told her. "I am not taking back my invitation, but I did not realize there might be so much pilikia. I believe you should think over the whole matter carefully before you decide to go."

"Instead of discouraging me, your latest news makes me want to tackle the mystery of Kaluakua all the more!"

The Hawaiian smiled. "I was hoping you

would say that," he told her. A moment later he arose to leave. "My very best wishes to you and all your party," he said.

After Mr. Sakamaki had left, Nancy once more telephoned to Bess and George. This time she found both of them at home and asked the two girls to come to the Drew house immediately. "Big adventure coming up," she told the cousins, who promised to hurry over.

They arrived at the Drew home the same time Nancy did. Bess, blond and slightly plump, dimpled as she smiled. "Is this adventure just for fun, or is it going to be full of hair-raising episodes like the other mysteries we've worked on together?"

"Whatever it is, I'm ready for something different," George remarked. She was tall and slender and wore her dark hair in a short casual cut. George, in contrast to her timid cousin Bess, was matter-of-fact and practical.

As soon as the girls entered the house, Nancy asked Hannah to come into the living room. After the four sat down, the young sleuth told about the proposed Hawaiian trip.

"Dreamy!" exclaimed Bess. "But it does sound dangerous."

"Hypers, I can hardly wait to go!" George remarked. "I hope our parents will let us."

Hannah Gruen wore a broad, contented smile. "Nancy," she said, "this is one time I can keep an eye on you while you're working on a mystery."

The three girls laughed. But Hannah's face suddenly clouded. "I don't know, though, whether it's safe to go out to that Pacific island. They have volcanoes out there that are apt to start up any minute. Then their food is so different!"

"Hannah dear," said Nancy, "it's high time you learned about our newest state of Hawaii. It is one of the most up-to-date places in the world and one of the most beautiful."

"I can tell you a few facts about Hawaii," George spoke up. "There are seven main islands on which people live. Honolulu is the capital and it's on Oahu. The population is made up mainly of pure Hawaiians, part Hawaiians, Caucasians, and Orientals. The most handsome people in the world live there."

Bess made a wry face at her cousin. "Well, you certainly have been reading up on it," she gibed. "And now I'm going to call home and get permission to go."

Her parents gladly consented, then George phoned her mother and father. She too was told she might make the trip.

As George announced this to the others, Bess suddenly gave a little squeal. "Girls, the boys are going out to Hawaii. Remember?"

"That's right," said George.

Nancy said she would put in a call at once to

Emerson College and talk to Ned, since his plane was leaving that night.

When Ned heard that the girls were going to Hawaii, he gave a loud whoop. "Nancy, this is the most wonderful news of the day! We fellows are leaving here in a little while. We're going first to California and then fly on from there. As soon as you girls arrive, we'll come out to Kaluakua. In the meantime, you'll find our gang at the Halekulani Hotel."

"That's on Waikiki Beach, isn't it?" Nancy asked.

"Yes, it is. And get there as fast as you can!"

After a few more minutes of conversation, in which Ned promised he would pass along the good word to Burt and Dave, he and Nancy said good-by. Then she turned to Hannah Gruen and the girls.

"Dad will get our reservations," she said. "He may pick up something in a hurry, so you'd better start packing."

Bess and George left at once to get started on their packing. Nancy and Hannah began looking over their own clothes for the trip.

During breakfast the next morning the telephone rang. Nancy answered it and learned to her surprise that the caller was the window washer, Abe Antok.

"I have an important message for you, miss,"

he said. "I don't want to give it to you on the phone 'cause somebody else may be listenin'. I'll be washin' windows at 37 Maple Street. Can you come over there and talk to me?"

Nancy promised to meet him in a short while. Eager to learn what Abe had to tell her, she finished her breakfast quickly and started out. On the way she met George, who was going downtown to buy a new bathing suit.

"Please come with me first," Nancy asked, and told her about Abe's message.

"All right," George agreed.

The two girls reached 37 Maple Street in ten minutes. As they approached the side of the house, closely planted with high bushes, they saw a ladder that extended to the second floor. Abe was at the top of it, busily washing a window.

As Nancy was about to call to him, the ladder began to sway. The next moment it was yanked away from the house!

Abe Antok, meanwhile, had grabbed for the window sill and now clung to it desperately, his legs hanging in mid-air. "Help!" he screeched.

At that moment Nancy spotted a man lurking among the bushes. He was holding onto the ladder. Suddenly he let it drop and dashed off through the back yard!

CHAPTER IV

A Rewarding Chase

For a brief second the eyes of the two girls were rooted to the sill of the second-floor window, from which Abe Antok hung, while the man who had caused the trouble was running away at top speed.

"Nancy, go after that man!" George ordered. "I'll help Abe."

Without a moment's hesitation, Nancy started through the back yard of 37 Maple Street. The window washer continued to call for help. The house owner heard him and opened the window. She grabbed Abe's hands, just as George set up the ladder. Abe rested his feet on one of the rungs. Panting from exertion, he thanked George and the house owner, who wanted to know what had happened.

Quickly George explained, adding, "I hope my friend Nancy Drew catches up with that awful man. Why, Abe, you might have been killed!"

Nancy, meanwhile, was pursuing the fugitive through gardens, streets, and driveways. She managed to keep him in sight, hoping all the time she would find a policeman to help in the chase. As she reached a cross street, a patrol car came along. Rushing up to it, she waved her arms. When the car stopped, she gasped:

"Officer, follow me quickly, please! I'm after a man who tried to kill somebody!"

The policeman seated beside the driver lost no time in alighting and following Nancy. As they ran, she explained what had happened.

Once they almost lost their quarry as he dashed around the corner of a building, but in a few moments they saw him again. He evidently was staying off the streets as much as possible to avoid being captured. Nancy and the officer ran even faster and presently closed in on the fugitive who was trying to climb a tall fence.

The policeman pulled him down.

"What d'you want me for?" the man asked. He was young, surly-looking, and had a shock of black hair which hung down over his forehead. "I ain't done nothin'."

As the officer held on to his prisoner, he said to Nancy, "This fellow is one of our town mischief-makers. He's the leader of a gang known as the Green Tigers. Come along, Jake. We'll go back to that place where you yanked the ladder away from the window washer."

The hoodlum stared unbelievingly. Apparently he had been so sure no one had seen him that he was startled into a confession.

"I didn't mean no harm. I was just havin' some fun."

"That's not fun," the officer said. "Come along!"

With Nancy leading the way, he prodded Jake along until they reached 37 Maple Street. By this time Abe was on the ground, talking with George and the house owner. As the prisoner was marched up to the group, Abe looked at him malevolently.

"So you're the guy who did it! What's the big idea?"

"It wasn't my idea," the hoodlum sniveled. "A man came to me and told me I was to watch you and try to make things hard for you."

"You didn't have to try to kill me!" Abe cried out. "Who was this man?"

"I don't know his name. He said he was goin' to blow town but somebody else was goin' to watch me. If I didn't carry out his orders, he'd see that I got in trouble with the police."

"What did this man look like?" Nancy asked.

"Oh, he was medium height—dark, thin, and not much hair on the top of his head."

Instantly Nancy realized that the description fitted Jim O'Keefe.

"Where did you meet him?" she asked Jake.

He said the man had come over to his table in a restaurant and talked to him.

"Did you notice anything unusual about the way he used his hands?" the young sleuth inquired.

Jake thought for a moment, then said, "Come to think of it, he did do something funny with his fingers. He'd kind of beat on the table, then he'd lift two of his fingers and make them meet."

Nancy turned to the policeman. "I think the name of the man is Jim O'Keefe, and that he's the thief who broke into our house."

At this announcement Jake's eyes opened wide. "You must be Nancy Drew! You're the one that got Abe here in trouble. It was because Abe talked too much to you. He was being shadowed. Well, this guy wanted me to make it hard for Abe."

"Yes, I am Nancy Drew. What else can you tell us about this Jim O'Keefe?"

Before answering, the hoodlum asked the policeman if things would go easier for him if he told what he knew. The officer said it was not up to him to decide that, but it certainly would be to his advantage to tell the truth.

"Well, this guy that you call O'Keefe," Jake said, "bragged about bein' the front man for a slick gang."

The officer had taken out a notebook and pencil and was making notes. He waited for Jake to go

on, but the hoodlum declared he had told all he
knew about O'Keefe.

The officer now addressed the window washer.
He asked if Abe knew Jake. The workman vig-
orously denied this and said haughtily, "I want
you to know, Officer, that I'm an honest man. I
do my work and take care of my family. I never
have anything to do with hoods."

The window washer admitted, however, that
the previous night he had received a mysterious
phone call. "I think the voice was the same one
as the man who rented the ladder. He told me
I was goin' to be punished for tellin' Nancy Drew
what I did. I called Miss Drew this morning and
asked her to come over, so that I could tell her this.
I was afraid she might be in some danger."

"I certainly appreciate your kindness," said
Nancy with a smile. "But, Abe, please be careful
yourself."

The policeman took Jake off in the patrol car.
Nancy and George walked to the next corner
where they parted.

"Watch your step!" George warned her chum
as she started toward the shopping area.

Upon reaching home, Nancy found Hannah
Gruen putting a large suitcase on a scales. The
housekeeper heaved a great sigh. "Can't take
this much. They'll charge extra on the plane."
Then she asked, "What did the window washer
want to tell you?"

When Nancy finished the story, the house-keeper gasped, "Oh, Nancy, you may be in terrible danger. Couldn't we just go to Honolulu without getting mixed up with a lot of underhanded people?"

Nancy gave Hannah an affectionate squeeze. "Let's not start worrying so early," she suggested. "But I guess what I'd better start worrying about is my own packing."

The young detective went into her bedroom, opened her closet door, and began selecting the dresses she would take.

"This white cotton will be good, and a couple of lightweight sweater suits," Nancy said to herself.

She also chose a yellow, a pale blue, and a red-and black-flowered sunback costume. Then her mind began to wander from the subject at hand.

"I believe I'll invite Mr. and Mrs. Sakamaki to dinner this evening," she told herself. "They probably know many Polynesian legends. They might be able to remember one that has to do with water or sleep or death."

She hurried to the telephone and called the Hawaiians. Both were delighted to accept the invitation and arrived promptly at seven o'clock. When Nancy brought up the subject of the legends, Mr. Sakamaki said:

"It's possible that the legend about Pele, the Sleeping Goddess of the Volcano, may help you.

According to the Islanders, Pele now sleeps a good deal, and awakens only once in a while to produce a volcano. But in ancient times she was very active. Some ten thousand years ago, while trying to find a permanent home on Oahu Island, she built two mountain peaks, Koko Head and Koko Crater from a great crack she caused in the Koolau Range. The legend goes on to say that the goddess was completely satisfied and went to sleep on the island.

"However, other stories are told that she sleeps in Kilauea Crater on Hawaii Island, but awakens to put on a fiery display at nearby Mauna Loa."

When dinner was over and everyone had gathered in the living room, Mr. Sakamaki asked if the Drews would mind turning on their television to the newscast to hear the weather forecast for the next day.

Nancy turned on the television set and tuned it to the proper channel. The telecast had barely started when the announcer electrified the Drews with a news bulletin which he said had just been received by the station.

"Word has come," he began, "of a plane in trouble over the Pacific. It is one which was chartered by a group of students from Emerson College."

"Oh, Dad!" Nancy cried out fearfully. "That's the plane that Ned and Dave and Burt are on!"

CHAPTER V

Double Worries

THE NEWS that the plane carrying the Emerson College boys over the Pacific was in trouble stunned Nancy. Mr. Drew, though fearful, tried to cheer his daughter by saying that pilots often accomplished miraculous feats with their craft. But as time went on even the lawyer had to admit that the reports were most discouraging.

"We mustn't give up hope, though," he said.

Mr. and Mrs. Sakamaki left in a little while. They expressed the fervent hope that the chartered plane would make a safe landing.

Nancy and her father, seated near Hannah Gruen, decided to turn on a radio, so they could get almost continuous reports.

"Do you think I should call Bess and George?" Nancy asked her father.

"Perhaps you shouldn't worry them," Mr. Drew replied.

The words were hardly out of his mouth when

the three heard footsteps on the front porch, then the ringing of the doorbell. Nancy hurried to answer.

"Bess! George!" she cried out.

"Oh, Nancy, you've heard the news?" Bess asked, her voice trembling.

Nancy nodded as the three girls walked into the living room. Bess and George spoke to Mr. Drew and Hannah Gruen, then sat down to look and listen to the television and radio. Hour after hour went by with everyone's hopes dimming. At dawn Mr. Drew suggested that the girls go to bed.

"I couldn't sleep," said Nancy.

"Nor I," George and Bess agreed simultaneously.

At that moment a radio announcer said, "We interrupt this program for a special bulletin. Word has just been received that the plane carrying the students from Emerson College has landed at the Los Angeles airport. Everyone is safe."

"Hypers!" George cried out.

"Oh, isn't that wonderful!" Nancy exclaimed.

Bess said nothing. Tears of joy stood in her eyes. But she joined in the jubilation which followed. Everyone hugged everyone else, and then Hannah hurried to the kitchen and prepared a snack consisting of hot chocolate and toast.

"And now for some sleep," said Nancy, yawning, as she put down her empty cup. "Girls, you'd better stay here."

"You won't have to ask me twice," George replied wearily. She telephoned home, and then Bess called her family.

While the girls were preparing for bed, Bess kept staring into space and had little to say. Finally Nancy asked her what the trouble was.

"Maybe I'm a sissy," her friend replied, "but after what happened to the boys I'm not sure I want to fly to Honolulu."

Nancy, catching a look of disdain in George's eyes quickly winked at her, then said, "After you've had a good sleep, Bess, I'm sure you'll feel better about the whole thing."

Nancy's prediction proved to be true. When Bess awakened in the late morning, she laughed at her own fears. "I wouldn't miss this trip for anything in the world," she declared.

Immediately after brunch the cousins left. Nancy decided to drive downtown and shop for another small suitcase. As she was about to leave the house, the telephone rang. Police Captain McGinnis was calling her.

"Would you mind coming down to my office?" he asked. "I think you'll be interested in something we've found out."

"I'll be there in a few minutes," the young sleuth answered.

When she reached police headquarters, Captain McGinnis told her that detectives had uncovered evidence which might link the thief who had entered her home to a rather unusual nation-wide gang.

"We don't actually know any of the members," the officer went on. "But we've been told they call themselves the Double Scorps."

"Double Scorps?" Nancy said. "Is there any special significance to that name?"

"It stands for Scorpions," Captain McGinnis replied. "From what we have found out, they always work in pairs and they're a bad lot."

He opened a large ledger-type book on his desk. "There are a number of unexplained local robberies on our blotter," he said. "One is of particular interest. A man's ancient Chinese ring of great value was taken from the home of Mr. Homer Milbank."

The officer looked up and smiled at Nancy. "I thought perhaps you'd like to help us," he said.

Nancy lifted her eyebrows. "Me? Captain McGinnis, you know I'm going to Honolulu."

"That's just the point," the officer told her. "Mr. Milbank bought the ring in Honolulu. There is just a possibility it may find its way back there. In any case, the *modus operandi* points to members of the Double Scorps gang."

"I see," said Nancy. "What did the ring look like?"

From his ledger Captain McGinnis took a photostat of a crude drawing of the ring. He said Mr. Milbank had had it made for the police. The officer handed the paper to Nancy who studied it closely for several seconds. Suddenly she leaned forward excitedly.

"Captain McGinnis," she began, "I'm familiar with two of these four symbols. They're not Chinese but Polynesian. Look at this one." She pointed. "It stands for water, and this other one indicates sleep or death."

It was the officer's turn to show amazement. "I knew I was asking the right person to help me," he said, grinning. "And I'd like to bet that you can tell me within a few hours what those other two symbols stand for."

Smiling, Nancy arose. "You may be right," she replied. "I'll even try to cut the time in half."

Leaving Captain McGinnis mystified, Nancy drove at once to the home of Professor Wharton and showed him the drawing.

After looking at the photostat a moment, he said that Nancy was correct in her supposition about all the symbols on the ring being Polynesian. "It probably was carved right in the Hawaiian Islands. These other two symbols stand for woman and tapa. You probably know that tapa is a cloth made from the bark of a variety of mulberry tree which grows on the Islands."

Nancy returned to police headquarters and reported to Captain McGinnis what she had learned.

"Fine work, Nancy," he said.

For several minutes the two discussed the odd fact that the ring was the only article stolen from the Milbank home.

In a teasing tone he said, "Of course I expect you to find the answer to that question."

Nancy stood up, saluted, and with a chuckle answered, "Aye, aye, Captain, I shall try my best!"

As she drove toward home, a sudden thought came to Nancy. Her dog Togo must be cared for while she and her father and Hannah were away!

"I'll take him to that lovely boarding home for dogs out in the country," she said to herself.

At home Nancy found a message from her father, saying he had secured reservations for two days later. Since the next day would be a busy one for her, she decided to take Togo to the boarding home at once.

Nancy called Togo. When he did not come, she asked the housekeeper where the terrier was.

"Why, I don't know," Hannah replied.

She and Nancy went outside. They whistled and called repeatedly. Still Togo did not come.

"But he never strays away from our property!" Nancy declared.

"No, never," Hannah agreed.

Nancy and the housekeeper stared at each other, worry in their eyes. Something must have happened to little Togo!

CHAPTER VI

A Disastrous Dance

"HANNAH, when did you last see Togo?" Nancy asked the housekeeper.

"Oh, about an hour ago. He barked to go outside and I let him."

Nancy hurried into the house to call the River Heights' dog pound. The warden there frequently cruised around the streets in a small caged truck and picked up stray dogs.

"Something might have lured Togo into the street and perhaps the dog warden took him away," Nancy said to herself.

But after she gave a full description of the little terrier, the warden informed her that the pet was not at the pound. Nancy began to worry more than ever. With a heavy heart she came outside again and told Hannah what she had learned.

"I'm going to ask our neighbors if any of them saw Togo," she said.

"Oh, I do hope you find him. Togo is such a dear and lots of company."

Nancy went from house to house. But one person after another gave her a negative reply. Finally, however, she got a clue from a little boy who was riding a tricycle.

"Sure I saw your dog," the lad said. "He went away in a car."

"A car?" Nancy asked. "Whose car?"

"I don't know," the boy answered. "It stopped in front of your house just before I rode past. A man got out and called to Togo. He was on your front lawn. The man had a bone and your dog came to get it. Then the man picked him up and took him away in the car."

Nancy was stunned. A dognaper! She asked the child what the man looked like, but he had not noticed his face.

"Don't *you* know who he was?" the boy asked.

"No, I don't," Nancy answered. "But whoever he is, he's a mean person."

"Did he steal Togo?" the little boy asked excitedly.

"I'm afraid so," Nancy replied sadly. "Well, thank you for the information, Tommy."

When she reached home, she said to Hannah, "I have a terrible feeling that one of the Double Scorps took Togo. Perhaps he hoped by doing this to keep us from going on the trip—or, at least, delay us."

During the afternoon Nancy made further inquiries and reported the incident to Captain McGinnis. But evening came and there still was no clue to the whereabouts of her stolen pet.

For the second night Nancy Drew slept but little. She and Togo were fast friends and the thought of perhaps losing him forever made her very unhappy. Then suddenly she sat up in bed. Had she heard a whine and a short bark, or had she imagined them both?

"No, I'm not dreaming!" Nancy said to herself, as she detected the sounds again.

Grabbing up a robe and slippers she quickly put them on and leaped down the front stairway two steps at a time. Then she raced to the kitchen door and opened it. Togo dashed in and she swept him up in her arms.

"Oh, you blessed little thing! You're back!" Nancy cried, hugging her pet. "How I wish you could talk and tell me who took you! But never mind. You're home now, and no dognaper will ever get you again!"

She noticed that both the terrier's license and collar were missing. She gave her pet an extra squeeze. "You broke loose and got away from that dreadful man, didn't you?" she asked.

Togo yipped and licked her face. She set him down and he ran over to his two special dishes in a corner of the kitchen. Thirstily, Togo lapped water from one, as Nancy filled the other with dog food. When he finished eating, Nancy picked him up and took him to her room.

"I'm going to watch over you personally!" she told Togo. He snuggled down in a boudoir chair. Nancy got into bed and instantly fell asleep.

She was up early the following morning, and when she came downstairs with Togo, both her father and Hannah Gruen looked at her and the dog in amazement. Nancy related what had happened. Neither Mr. Drew nor the housekeeper had heard Togo the night before!

As soon as Nancy finished eating breakfast and had helped Hannah with the dishes, she drove off with her pet to the boarding home for dogs. On the drive back, as she passed the home of Mr. and Mrs. Sakamaki, she decided to stop and tell them that she was leaving the next day for Hawaii.

As she walked toward the front door, she heard strains of a guitar coming from the sunroom at the side of the house. Glancing through the window, she saw Mr. Sakamaki strumming a large guitar. He was wearing a gay flowered shirt, and an orchid *lei* hung about his neck. His wife, dressed in an embroidered, long, loose-fitting gown, which Nancy recognized as the Hawaiian *muumuu*, was going through the graceful motions of a hula dance.

Nancy hesitated. Should she call just now or come back later? As she was debating whether or not to ring the bell, the door suddenly opened.

Mrs. Sakamaki stood there and at once invited Nancy inside, saying she had seen her from the window.

"But I don't want to intrude if you are busy," Nancy said quickly.

"We are only having our morning exercise," Mrs. Sakamaki replied. "Perhaps," she added, as her husband came forward, "you would like to join us—even learn to dance the hula."

Mr. Sakamaki heartily approved his wife's suggestion. He said he thought Nancy would enjoy knowing the Hawaiian dance.

"I'd love to learn the hula," Nancy answered. "I hope I shan't appear awkward."

"You are very graceful, Nancy. You will learn easily," Mrs. Sakamaki assured her.

"But before we start the lesson," said her husband, "perhaps our guest has some news for me?"

Nancy replied that she and her friends were leaving for Hawaii the next day. Then she told him about the dognaping episode and her suspicion that the person who had taken Togo was trying to prevent her from going on the trip.

"It does seem to prove that he wants to keep you away from Kaluakua," Mr. Sakamaki agreed. "You must be very careful while you are there."

Mrs. Sakamaki now led the way into the sunroom, where her husband picked up the guitar. As Nancy waited for the hula lesson to begin, she glanced around.

The small room was decorated almost completely with Chinese articles. In the center of the room stood a low tea table on which were an exquisite set of china cups, saucers, and a teapot. Nearby on a teakwood stand was a fine handmade model of a large outrigger canoe with a tapa canopy. When Mr. Sakamaki noticed Nancy looking at it, he said, "That piece is very old. An antique."

"It is very lovely," Nancy remarked, thinking that she must be careful during the dancing lesson not to bump into any of the art pieces in the room.

"Shall we start?" Mrs. Sakamaki asked.

Her husband began to play a lovely Hawaiian melody. Nancy watched Mrs. Sakamaki's feet carefully and soon was imitating the side-to-side step. Next came the swaying of the body, and finally, Mrs. Sakamaki demonstrated the graceful raising and lowering of the arms and head.

"With our hands and fingers we express certain ideas," Mrs. Sakamaki explained to her pupil. "For instance, move your hands forward together as if extending a gift. But do it with a slight rolling motion."

The lesson went on for some time. Both Mr. and Mrs. Sakamaki praised Nancy's progress highly. They said that with a little practice and a proper costume, she could easily join a Hawaiian group.

Nancy felt pleased. In her enthusiasm to indicate various ideas with her arms and hands, she forgot about the smallness of the room and its many art objects. *Suddenly one arm swept the antique outrigger canoe from its stand!*

Nancy made a wild dive to keep it from falling on the china teapot and cups. Although she managed to deflect the canoe, so that it missed the dishes, she was unable to prevent it from crashing to the floor.

"Oh, dear!" she exclaimed, and bent to pick up the model.

To her horror, it was rather badly damaged. The outrigger had broken off, as well as the uprights which held the tapa. "I'm dreadfully sorry!"

Mr. Sakamaki made light of the matter. Both he and his wife said they were glad Nancy herself was all right. The canoe could be mended.

The couple persuaded Nancy to practice the hula for another half hour. By this time she had begun to feel at ease in the swaying, relaxing rhythm of the Hawaiian dance. Before saying good-by, she mentioned the damaged canoe once more, offering to pay for the repair work.

"I shall probably repair it myself," Mr. Sakamaki said. "Please do not worry any more about it."

Nancy heaved a sigh. Smiling, she said, "But

The valuable antique toppled from the stand

because of it, I shall work all the harder to solve the mystery at Kaluakua."

She was about to leave the house when Mr. Sakamaki answered the ringing telephone. Upon learning who the caller was, he asked Nancy to wait. He wrote down a message, then hung up and turned to Nancy.

"That was an answer to my telegram to friends, Mr. and Mrs. Armstrong, in Honolulu. They will meet you at the airport and drive you to Kaluakua."

"That was most kind of you," said Nancy.

The Hawaiian gave a broad smile. "Mrs. Sakamaki and I thought you should know people in Honolulu on whom you could call in case of trouble. The Armstrongs are our closest friends."

"You think of everything," Nancy said gratefully. "It will be so nice having the Armstrongs meet us."

After saying good-by again, she drove directly home. As she pulled into the driveway Nancy was surprised to see the Drews' housekeeper standing there waiting for her. She looked very pale and Nancy suspected that something had happened.

"Oh, Hannah, you have bad news?" she asked.

"I'm afraid so," the housekeeper replied.

CHAPTER VII

A Studio Accident

WORRIED, Nancy stood tensely, waiting for the housekeeper to continue.

"It's about your father," Hannah Gruen began.

"Oh, has he been hurt?" Nancy cried out fearfully.

Sympathetically the woman put an arm around the girl's shoulders. "Yes, dear. But Mr. Drew is very fortunate," Hannah went on, "not to have been injured more severely. He was attacked in his office by an unknown assailant."

"How dreadful!" Nancy cried out. "Tell me what happened," she urged as Hannah paused a moment.

"Your father was seated at his desk. He heard the door open and thought it was his secretary, who was late. Instead, a masked man with a hat pulled low over his forehead rushed in and attacked your father. He fought back, but suddenly his assailant gave him a hard blow which knocked him out. He was unconscious when his secretary found him."

"How horrible!" Nancy exclaimed. "Where is Dad now?"

Hannah said he was in the hospital. The doctor who had been called in had insisted he be taken there and remain quiet for a while.

"I must go to Dad at once!" Nancy said. "Which hospital, Hannah?"

"River Heights General."

Nancy hurried to the hospital. Upon inquiry, she learned that her father was in Room 782. Her heart pounding, Nancy went up in the elevator and walked swiftly down the hall.

The door to Room 782 was open. Mr. Drew was in bed, propped up with pillows.

"Oh, Dad!" Nancy murmured, kissing him lightly.

"Now don't worry, honey." Her father smiled wanly. "I'm really all right. That doctor just wants to make a checkup."

"Well, I'm glad you're all right," said Nancy. But her eyes traveled to the several bruises on her father's cheeks and forehead, and she thought his eyes seemed to glisten more than usual. He probably was feverish, she decided.

"I'm glad you came, honey," the lawyer said. "Of course this little scrap I got into means I'll have to postpone my trip to Honolulu."

"Never mind," Nancy consoled him. "I won't leave yet, either. The mystery of Kaluakua can wait."

"I'm afraid it can't," Mr. Drew replied. "My attacker said something which I believe makes it imperative for you and the others to go ahead without me and start solving the mystery."

The lawyer explained that just before he had lost consciousness from the knockout blow, his assailant had remarked acidly, "Maybe this will keep you on the mainland!"

Nancy's jaw set. "It seems to prove that your assailant is one of the Double Scorps."

Her father nodded. "I'm sorry that I didn't get a look at his face. In fact, it was when I tried to, that he gave me the final blow. All I can tell you is, he wore a gray tweed suit.

"Nancy, I wish you would go to my office and see if you can pick up any clues. The police were notified and they are probably there." Mr. Drew smiled fondly at his daughter. "Maybe you can give them a little help."

Nancy agreed to go at once and return to the hospital later. She hurried to the lawyer's office and found his secretary, Miss Robertson, on the verge of hysterics.

"Oh, Nancy, how is he?" the young woman cried out.

"Dad's really feeling pretty well," Nancy replied. "Please tell me your story."

Miss Robertson said that she had been late getting in that morning. When she arrived, the door to Mr. Drew's private office was ajar. "I sorted the mail and started to carry it in to your father's desk," she said. "And there—there he was, lying on the floor!"

"So you didn't see his attacker?" Nancy asked.

"No. He'd gone before I got here."

Nancy walked into her father's office. She was greeted by two police detectives whom she knew. One was busy taking fingerprints but said he felt sure Mr. Drew's assailant had not touched any of the furniture. The other man was examining the carpet with a magnifying glass, trying to distinguish the stranger's footprints from those of other persons.

"I'm afraid this isn't going to be of much help," he said finally, standing up.

Nancy, meanwhile, had been walking around the edge of the room, her eyes alert for any clue that the stranger unwittingly might have left. Finally she asked, "Is it all right for me to walk in the center of the room now?"

When the detective nodded, she began a search of chairs, table, bookcase, window sills, and desk. Between two papers on her father's desk, she found a small piece of tweed cloth.

"I may have a clue!" she told the men excitedly.

Nancy called Miss Robertson into the room

and asked her if any papers had been scattered on the floor when she found Mr. Drew there.

"Oh, yes," the secretary replied. "They were all over the place. I picked them up and put them on your father's desk."

Nancy turned to the detectives. "I believe this piece of tweed may have been torn from the coat of the man who attacked my father," she said.

One of them put the scrap of cloth in an envelope and dropped it into his pocket. "I guess your father pulled it from the fellow's coat. It may be a big help to us."

Nancy left the office and returned to the hospital. After reporting the latest finding to her father, she asked him when he would be able to make the Hawaiian trip.

"Oh, I'll follow you in a few days," he said cheerily.

"But you'll be home alone," Nancy protested.

Mr. Drew, realizing how worried his daughter was that he might be attacked again, promised her he would not stay alone. "I'll move down to the club for a few nights," he said.

Nancy made two more trips to the hospital that day, but there was no further news about Mr. Drew's attacker.

Early the next morning Mr. Marvin drove Bess, George, and their suitcases in the family station wagon to the Drew home. Nancy and Hannah climbed in and the travelers set off for the airport.

It was a perfect day for flying and within an hour Nancy and her friends were winging their way across the United States toward California.

"We're actually above the clouds," remarked Bess, who was seated next to the window. "I can't see any land below us."

"At this altitude you wouldn't see much, anyway," spoke up George, seated beside her cousin. "We're flying pretty high."

Nancy's seatmate was a beautiful young woman who had slept most of the time. She awoke as luncheon was served on trays fastened into the armrests. After lunch she chatted with the girls. Learning that they were on their way to Honolulu, she asked:

"Are you stopping over at Los Angeles?"

"Yes, we are," replied Nancy. "For several hours in fact. We're taking the night plane across the Pacific."

"If you have no plans," said the young woman, who had introduced herself as Sue Rossiter, "I have a suggestion of something interesting you might do—watch a movie being filmed. First, I should tell you that I'm an actress. The Bramley studio, where I work, is about to start filming a picture. It's a fantasy. I play the lead, a mermaid off Waikiki Beach."

"What an interesting part!" remarked Nancy, smiling.

Sue Rossiter went on to say that the interior scenes for the picture would be made in the studio. "But the outdoor scenes," she added, "are actually going to be shot at Waikiki."

To Nancy's disappointment, she learned that the movie company would not make the Hawaiian trip for some time. By then the visitors from River Heights probably would have left the Islands.

But the actress said, "Why don't you come to the studio? I'll see that you have passes."

"We'd love to," said Nancy. She glanced intently at her seatmate for a moment, then added, "Isn't your stage name Fran Johnson?"

The young woman laughed and nodded. "I'll be expecting you at the studio."

When the plane reached Los Angeles, the actress was met by a young man and driven off at once. After Hannah Gruen and the three girls had checked their baggage on the Honolulu plane, Nancy wired Ned to inform him which flight they were taking. Then the four took a taxi to the Bramley studio. They had not gone far on the boulevard when Bess, looking out the rear window, insisted that they were being followed.

"How can you tell in this heavy traffic?" George chided her cousin from the front seat.

Nancy had already glanced back too. "Bess could be right," she said, and leaned forward to tell the driver their suspicions. "Would it be possible for you to throw the car behind us off our trail?" she asked.

"Why sure, miss," the driver replied. With a broad grin, he added, "We've got to protect our visitors."

The taximan had no trouble eluding the car. He took a circuitous route, but finally pulled up in front of the Bramley studio. Fran Johnson was waiting for them at the door. "Hurry!" she urged. "The author of the script is going to explain a legend in it to a group of company executives. I think you'll find it interesting."

She led the way into a small auditorium, motioned the girls to seats, and then left them. A young man, standing before a seated group, was saying:

"How much is fact and how much is legend we do not know. But it's said that the first inhabitants of the Hawaiian Islands were Polynesians who came from other Pacific islands, particularly Tahiti. They landed from enormous outrigger canoes. Their favorite landing spot was Waikiki Beach. They preferred to come in on the surf in their shallow canoes rather than land in calmer waters. That is why we have chosen this beach for our story. It takes place about a thousand years ago. And now, ladies and gentlemen, suppose we proceed directly with the rehearsal."

Nancy and her friends followed the others through the building to a large sound stage.

Warning signs for absolute silence were posted in several places. Great ceiling lights, manipulated by men on high platforms, flooded the scene. Cameramen seated on small trucks carrying their equipment dollied back and forth for proper shots.

Nancy, Bess, George, and Hannah took seats in a row behind the chairs where the director, the author, and two executives had sat down. The first scene to be shot was laid just outside an ancient thatch-roofed hut. A young Polynesian actor stepped from the doorway and listened intently.

"That strange sound on the water again," he said softly.

At that moment the great light focused directly on him went out and someone called, "Cut!"

While waiting for the light to be repaired, the young actor walked over toward the director. Fran Johnson approached Nancy and was just about to speak to her when their attention was diverted to a great boom carrying a workman. Apparently he was an electrician. The boom swung toward the light which had gone out. As everyone looked upward, the heavy steel arm suddenly hit another huge light.

There was a resounding crash and a shower of glass came down toward those below!

CHAPTER VIII

The Surprising Clue

THE studio visitors made a mad scramble for safety. Chairs were overturned and electric cords tripped over as Nancy and the others scurried in every direction. They were not a second too soon. Pieces of glass and metal crashed to the floor and sprayed out for several feet.

"O-o-oh!" Bess cried, catching her breath. "Let's go before something else happens."

"Oh, don't be a sissy," George spoke up. "I want to see some more filming."

But George's desire was not to be fulfilled. The actors and actresses had had such a fright that all of them declared they could not work any more that day. The director acceded to their wishes, and postponed the rehearsal to the next day.

Fran Johnson came to say good-by to the girls. "I'm dreadfully sorry about what happened, but you'll soon see Waikiki Beach for real and you'll find plenty of thatch-roofed huts on the Islands."

Nancy smiled. "And when the picture is released, we'll certainly go to see it."

They thanked Fran for inviting them to the studio, then, with Hannah, took a taxi to the airport. Upon arriving there, Nancy glanced at her watch. "We have lots of time. I think I'll call Dad and find out out how he is."

While the others waited, she went to a telephone booth and put in a person-to-person call to Mr. Drew at the River Heights General Hospital. Presently she was told by the operator that Mr. Drew was not there, so she gave the number of his club. A few moments later her father answered.

"Good to hear from you, Nancy," he said cheerfully. "I know you're going to ask me why I'm not in the hospital. Well, the truth is, the doctor has discharged me. I'm feeling fine. He won't let me start the trip for a couple of days, though. I promised to stay right here and rest."

Nancy laughed. "I know you, Dad. You'll rest by staying on the telephone talking to clients or writing briefs."

"Well, you wouldn't want me to die of lonesomeness without you, would you?" Mr. Drew teased. Then he became serious. "Nancy, I have some good news for you. That scrap of tweed cloth you found in my office proved to be a valuable clue. The police have nabbed the hoodlum who attacked me."

"Oh, how wonderful!" Nancy exclaimed. "Who was he?"

"The man belongs to the same gang of hoodlums as the ladder snatcher, who is under arrest. This fellow was also hired by O'Keefe to cause trouble."

Nancy asked her father if there was any report on O'Keefe himself. "Yes. The man who knocked me out corroborated the other fellow's story. O'Keefe has skipped town. This second prisoner says he has left the U. S. mainland."

"For the Hawaiian Islands?" Nancy asked.

"No one knows. He did not divulge his destination," the lawyer replied. "The hoodlum said that O'Keefe was a collector of old jewelry and other small antique pieces. Apparently he 'collects' them without paying for them." Mr. Drew laughed softly. "O'Keefe told the hoodlum that he had a special market for the pieces, but he didn't say what it was."

Father and daughter chatted a few minutes longer. Both felt sure O'Keefe had stolen Mr. Milbank's ring. Then, with an affectionate "See you soon, Dad," Nancy hung up. She rejoined her friends who were amazed to hear the latest news about O'Keefe.

Hannah Gruen frowned. "I have a dreadful feeling that man is going to make more trouble for all of us," she said. "I don't know that as a chaperon I can cope with the situation properly."

Nancy patted the housekeeper on the shoulder. "Please don't worry, Hannah," she begged. "You know all of us have been in tight spots before. We can handle this one!" she stated confidently.

A short time later the travelers boarded the overseas plane. Their seats were on opposite sides of the aisle but directly across from one another. Soon the fascinating Los Angeles sky line was receding in the distance. When darkness came, Hannah and the girls stretched out for a night's sleep.

They awakened to a gorgeous sunrise which followed them for a long time. Finally the Hawaiian Islands came into view. Up above them floated rose-tinted clouds and here and there the travelers could see a mountain peak. Below, palm trees waved in the gentle morning breeze.

The great plane landed smoothly. Nancy and her friends stepped out, and began looking around for Mr. and Mrs. Armstrong. How could they ever find them, they wondered, in the mass of people awaiting the visitors? The arms of men and women were laden with colorful flower leis.

As the girls went through the gate, a smiling couple walked up to Nancy. "Are you Nancy Drew?" the woman asked pleasantly.

"Yes, I am. And you must be Mrs. Armstrong."

The woman nodded as Mr. Armstrong introduced himself. At the same time the couple began slipping leis over the shoulders of the River Heights group. For Nancy there was one of white gardenias, a favorite flower of hers.

"Thank you so very much," she said. "This is a wonderful greeting!"

There was no chance for any further conversation, for at that moment three young men rushed up to the girls.

"Ned!" cried Nancy, as her tall, dark-haired handsome friend came toward her.

"Burt!" George called to the blond, husky youth.

"Dave!" exclaimed Bess in delight, looking up at the rangily-built, green-eyed young man.

The Emerson boys' arms also held leis which they dropped around the girls' necks with quick kisses. Nancy's lei was made of pale-pink plumiera, George's of baby anthuriums, and Bess's of orchids and carnations.

Warm greetings were exchanged and Nancy introduced the Armstrongs. As the group walked into the airport building to claim the travelers' luggage, Bess insisted that they were being followed.

"Not again!" George wailed.

Bess was adamant. "I just know those two men I saw looking at us are members of the Double Scorps," she whispered to Nancy. "They've gone now."

Ned overheard the remark and wanted to know

what she meant by Double Scorps. Nancy explained quickly, adding that Bess might be right.

"Then we're going to throw those snoopers off the trail!" Ned declared. "Suppose we all go to the Halekulani where we fellows are staying. We'll have a swim and maybe a sail. Those Scorps will think you've changed your plans. Later on we'll drive out to Kaluakua."

Mr. and Mrs. Armstrong were agreeable to this plan and the whole group piled into their big sedan. As the travelers rode through the city of Honolulu, they were intrigued with the hustle and bustle of the modern capital of the Islands. Streams of people poured into tall office buildings and department stores. Here and there, palm trees, waving in the soft breeze, shaded the sidewalks from the tropical sun.

Presently, Mr. Armstrong stopped the car and pointed to the dark-colored statue of a man atop a high, square pedestal. "That is a likeness of King Kamehameha, first king of all the Hawaiian Islands. Before that, each island had its own king."

Mr. Armstrong led the group to Iolani Palace nearby. Smiling, he said, "You know, this is the only palace in the United States."

As they went inside the cool, stately, high-ceilinged building, he explained that parts of the palace were now used by the legislative branch of the government.

"But the throne room looks exactly as it did many years ago, although the throne and the chairs on either side of it are replicas. The originals are in the Bishop Museum."

The visitors gazed at the beautiful paintings and draperies, conjuring up in their minds the grandeur of a bygone day when King Kamehameha had been seated on the throne in a gorgeous feather robe and headgear.

"And now I think we had better go," said Mr. Armstrong, and led the way back to his car.

A little while later they came to the Waikiki Beach area of Honolulu and turned into the driveway of an attractive garden which formed the grounds of the Halekulani Hotel.

They parked in front of the main building and Ned ran in to the office to ask for another room for the boys to use that day. They had insisted that the girls use their private apartment in one of the cottages with its lovely *lanai*.

Small suitcases belonging to Nancy, Bess, and George were carried to the first-floor apartment on the shady, flower-shrubbed grounds.

"We'll meet you girls on the beach in fifteen minutes," Ned said as the boys left them.

The girls changed to bathing suits, then went to the front of the hotel which faced the ocean. Mr. and Mrs. Armstrong and Hannah Gruen were seated on the tree-shaded terrace. Three feet below them stretched the white, sandy beach.

"How absolutely heavenly!" Bess exclaimed.

Mrs. Armstrong warned the girls that the tropi cal sunshine was very intense. She handed Nancy a bottle of suntan lotion and advised, "Better cover yourselves with this."

Nancy and her friends had just finished spraying themselves with the lotion when Ned, Burt, and Dave appeared. As they walked down to the water the visitors were fascinated by the surfboard riders a little distance away and by the twin-hulled sailboats with their gay-colored sails.

"I want you girls to go out in one of those catamarans," said Ned. "But let's swim first."

The six young people thoroughly enjoyed diving through the waves, swimming out a distance, and riding back in on the combers. Presently a catamaran with a red mainsail and a yellow jib pulled into the beach.

Ned spoke to the man at the tiller and the group climbed aboard. They sailed about half a mile out, then turned toward Diamond Head. From this vantage point, the mainlanders could get a fine view of Waikiki Beach, with its skyscraper hotels, beautiful gardens, and fine homes.

When they turned back toward the beach, George suggested that they all swim ashore. Nancy and Ned, the last to leave the catamaran, thanked the boat's owner for a fine sail, then headed for the beach. Reaching it, the pair sat down to dry off and talk.

"Tell me in detail about your trip," Nancy requested. "Just what did happen to the plane?"

"Actually, I'm not sure," Ned answered, "but I had a feeling we were never in any great danger. The radio went dead, so of course we had no communication with any airports. First one of our engines conked out, then another. At this point the pilot decided that the best thing to do would be to turn back.

"While we were waiting at the Los Angeles airport for the motors to be put in shape again, something rather unusual happened, Nancy. A man came up and asked if he might join our group."

Ned went on to say that the man explained he had missed the commercial flight to Honolulu and it was imperative he get to the Islands as soon as possible. "His papers and identification were in order, so there was no reason to refuse him. But, somehow, I didn't like him. Nancy, he had a habit of drumming on window sills, chair arms, and tables with his finger tips. It made us nervous."

Hearing this, Nancy sat up very straight. Looking at Ned intently, she asked, "And did this man raise his forefingers and touch them together?"

It was Ned's turn to look surprised. "Yes, he did, Nancy. For Pete's sake, how did you know that?"

CHAPTER IX

The Golden Pavilion

QUICKLY Nancy gave Ned full details regarding the thief who had stolen Mr. Drew's brief case. Ned in turn furnished a description of the man who had begged a ride on the Emerson plane.

"I'm sure he's Jim O'Keefe," Nancy stated.

"But he used the name of Tim O'Malley," Ned told her. "All his papers, tickets, and identifications were made out in that name."

"I wonder if O'Malley is his real name or an alias," Nancy mused. "Anyway, we know he's in the islands of Hawaii. Let's hope we can trap him."

"From all you tell me," Ned said, "this fellow sounds dangerous. I'm glad I'll be around to help you nab him."

Nancy decided that as soon as she was dressed she would put in a telephone call to River Heights. She told Ned that she wanted to tell her father about this latest development and ask his advice.

"But let's have a short sail and another swim first," Ned suggested.

They walked across the beach to the others, who were eager for another sail.

George said with a chuckle, "Once the mystery starts breaking at Kaluakua, we'll be kept hopping, with no time for water sports."

"I'm sure it won't be that bad," Nancy said, smiling. "I'll give you sleuths a few hours a day for fun."

"Oh, thanks so much," Dave said with an exaggerated bow.

The six young people swam out to a catamaran and climbed aboard. Soon they were whipping along once more toward Diamond Head.

"I wish we had some of this breeze in River Heights," George spoke up presently. "It seems to me that every time I go sailing on the Muskoka River at home the wind dies down and leaves me stranded."

"Oh, well, there's one thing we can brag about," Bess said loyally. "You can't beat the ice skating on our river."

When the sailboat returned to the area in front of the Halekulani, Dave asked, "Anybody want to dive in and race to shore?"

"Not in this balmy surf," Bess answered. "I'll race you in colder water some time."

The whole group swam leisurely to the beach and joined Hannah Gruen and the Armstrongs. Nancy told of her decision to telephone her father.

"Suppose we all meet in half an hour for luncheon," Mr. Armstrong suggested.

Nancy placed the call as soon as she reached the apartment the girls were using. Then, while waiting for the call to come through, she dressed. Twenty minutes later the telephone rang.

"Dad!" Nancy exclaimed joyfully. "Oh, it's good to hear your voice. How are you?"

Mr. Drew assured her that he was almost completely recovered. "I'll be able to start out on the trip soon," he said. "But some things have come up which will keep me in California longer than I planned, so I shan't be able to join you as quickly as I had hoped."

Nancy told him of the presence of Jim O'Keefe, alias Tim O'Malley, in Honolulu. The lawyer said he would pass along the information to Police Captain McGinnis and to Mr. Sakamaki.

"And do be careful," Mr. Drew begged his daughter. "The police here have picked up a few more reports on the Double Scorps. They're a dangerous gang."

"I promise," said Nancy. "But please don't worry. Mr. and Mrs. Armstrong are ready to help, and of course the three boys will be around all the time."

"I'm glad of that," replied Mr. Drew. "Mr. Sakamaki gave me a message for you. He said that while he would like the mystery solved, most important of all, he hopes you and the others will have a good time at Kaluakua."

"I'm sure we shall," said Nancy. "Best of luck on your journey, Dad. I'll be looking for you."

She said good-by, then relayed the messages to Bess and George. Bess looked a little frightened. "I don't like this Double Scorps business. Maybe we ought to stay here at the hotel and just go out to Kaluakua in the daytime to work on the mystery."

Nancy shook her head. "Not me. If you want to remain here, Bess, all right, but I'm going right out there and be on the spot when things happen. And don't forget, there may be a lot of sleuthing to do—even at night."

"And," added George, winking at Nancy over Bess's head, "ghosts never walk in the daytime and we want to find the one who dances at night."

Bess looked startled for a moment, then realized that her cousin was teasing. "Oh, I'll go of course," she said.

The three girls joined the rest of the party in the open-air restaurant. From their table they had a lovely view of the water, the beautiful flower gardens, and the enormous hau tree which stood to one side.

The visitors enjoyed a first course of ripe, sliced

pineapple, then, for a main dish, had delicious *mahimahi*, a native fish. During the meal, Ned suggested that the boys rent a car which they could use out at Kaluakua.

"You mean we may have to make a quick get-away?" George asked with a twinkle.

"You never can tell," Ned replied. "And also, we'll need it to run into town on errands."

The others thought Ned's idea of renting a car a good one, so the three boys went off with Mr. Armstrong to make arrangements. An hour later they returned with a salmon-colored convertible.

"Oh, it's yummy!" Bess called out from the hotel porch where the group was waiting. "Ned, you'll want to take it home with you."

"I'm afraid I will," said the young man, who was grinning from ear to ear. "Climb in, girls."

The six friends stepped into the convertible. Hannah rode with the Armstrongs. Ned followed Mr. Armstrong through the attractive, tree-shaded streets, and then along a shore drive. Half an hour later he turned into a driveway lined with hibiscus bushes in full bloom.

In the distance they could see a two-story white concrete mansion with a large columned front porch. In front of the house were croton bushes with varicolored leaves and near the driveway stood two royal poinciana trees with flaming red flowers.

"This is just heavenly," declared Bess, as Ned

stopped the car in front of the house and she stepped out.

From across a green lawn came a middle-aged man and a woman. He was short and dark, she blond and tall. They came up to the visitors and bowed.

"I am Kiyabu and at your service," the man said. "Welcome to Kaluakua. I hope your stay here will be very pleasant." He motioned for the woman to come forward. "This is my wife, Emma."

Emma, who said she was a New Englander, shook hands with the newcomers and told them everything was ready for their stay. She would show the visitors to their rooms while Kiyabu took care of the baggage.

Hannah and the girls followed the woman inside the spacious house, exquisitely furnished with Oriental pieces and draperies. Emma explained that she and her husband lived in a small cottage on the grounds not far from the main house.

"There is telephone service, and please call us whenever we can help you," she added.

In answer to a question from Bess, she told the mainlanders that Kiyabu was half Polynesian and half Japanese. "He is very proud of Kaluakua. Whenever you would like a tour of the grounds, he will be glad to take you." She smiled. "I'm sure you are eager to see the Golden Pavilion."

"Indeed we are," said Nancy.

"In the meantime," Emma went on, "I shall start preparing dinner. Hawaiians usually eat rather late, but maybe you would like to set your own dinner hour."

"I think that while we are here," Hannah Gruen spoke up, "we should follow the customs of the Hawaiians."

Soon the bags were brought upstairs, and after unpacking, the young people joined Kiyabu for a stroll around the sprawling grounds of Kaluakua. The estate included a tennis court and a fine stretch of bathing beach on which lay an outrigger canoe. Screened from the house and set in a beautiful private garden, not far from the water, was the Golden Pavilion. The visitors gazed at it in awe.

"I have never seen a more beautiful pavilion," said Nancy, entranced, as they came close to it.

The black-and-gold tile platform, hacked in a few places down to its concrete subfloor, was about three feet from the ground. Latticework of wood over concrete painted white circled the building below the floor. It had a diameter of some twenty feet. Short flights of steps led up to the platform on two sides.

The golden columns which supported the roof were round and glistened in the sunlight. The roof itself, completely of gold, was patterned in the graceful shape of a plumiera flower.

"It looks like an Oriental temple," George remarked.

"And so artistic," Bess spoke up admiringly. Recalling that Nancy had suggested it might have been erected over a grave and was lovely enough to be a memorial, she said, "Somebody *must* be buried beneath it."

Kiyabu smiled. "But not anyone human," he said. "However, it might be a grave of one of the helpers of the Queen of Sharks."

Startled by this remark, the others looked at Kiyabu for a further explanation. "You have never heard the story of ancient Pearl Harbor?" he asked. When they replied no, he went on:

"The Hawaiian name for Pearl Harbor is Puuloa, and the old Polynesians had a legend that it was the home of the Queen of the Sharks. Her name was Kaahupahau. She was a very kindly shark and lived in a place built in a cavern on the Honolulu side of Pearl Harbor.

"She loved the human race and ordered her shark people never to attack them. Part of their work was to keep man-eating sharks away from this whole area. The people who lived around were very friendly to these sharks and it is even said they sometimes rode on their backs."

Bess gave a little shudder. "It's a lovely story, but just the same I wouldn't want to meet a shark out in these waters."

Kiyabu was about to reply to this when he

turned quickly and looked toward the beach. No one was on it, but a worried look came over the Hawaiian's face.

"Is something wrong?" Nancy asked him quickly.

Kiyabu shrugged, but as the group started walking back to the house, he fell behind to talk to Nancy and Ned. "I heard strange whistling," he explained.

"Yes, I heard it too," said Nancy.

"I do not like it," said Kiyabu. "It may mean trouble. The other day Emma and I heard the same whistling on the beach. We went to investigate, but could find no one. When we returned to our cottage, it had been ransacked."

"You were robbed?" said Nancy. "How unfortunate!"

"That's the funny part of it." Kiyabu frowned. "Nothing was taken, but the intruder certainly was looking for something. Our house was a shambles."

"Have you any idea what he was looking for?" Ned asked him.

The caretaker said no, but he was sure it had something to do with the mystery of Kaluakua. Nancy asked Kiyabu if he thought perhaps the recent claimants to the estate might have been there hunting for something to help them prove their case.

"Who knows?" Kiyabu said noncommittally.

"But there is something else which I think you should know. Not long before Mr. Sakamaki Sr. died, a number of small valuable articles disappeared from the house—statuettes, some of them copies of old Polynesian pieces, and others that were genuine antiques from the Orient.

"Emma and I were greatly disturbed when we discovered that they were missing," Kiyabu went on. "I asked Mr. Sakamaki about them, but he just smiled at me. 'They are safe, Kiyabu,' he said. "But the executors have not been able to find any of them."

"It certainly sounds as if they had been stolen," Ned declared.

Kiyabu did not agree. "Mr. Sakamaki was very ill, but he managed to keep good account of everything. I'm sure he told me the truth when he said the items were safe. But where are they? The old gentleman was not strong enough to carry them outside the house and bury them."

Nancy was quiet for a few moments, then suggested, "Perhaps Mr. Sakamaki had a visitor and gave the pieces to him."

"Either that, or the person stole them and warned the old man not to say anything," Ned remarked.

Suddenly Kiyabu's eyes narrowed and his jaws set. "Maybe it was the man who brought the odd fish," he declared.

CHAPTER X

A Daytime Ghost

"TELL us about this man and the strange fish," Nancy urged Kiyabu.

The Hawaiian described the fish as being only a few inches long, with rough, scaleless skin. Because of its color and mottled markings the fish blends with the seaweed where it lives, and its paired fins enable the creature to climb about.

"This frogfish," Kiyabu went on, "has a great mouth, and on the snout above it is a slender 'rod' with a flap at the tip. The frogfish uses this as bait to lure the shrimp he eats."

Kiyabu said that the man who had brought the fish in a covered bucket was Mr. Ralph Emler. "Mr. Sakamaki asked him to stay to lunch and I served them," the caretaker continued. "Later I was sent into Honolulu to find a proper aquarium for the fish. When I returned, Mr. Emler had gone. The fish lived only a few hours. And it was not until the next day when Emma was dusting that she missed the statuettes."

"Please describe Mr. Emler," Nancy requested.

The caretaker told her that he was tall, with reddish-blond hair, and had a deep voice.

"Do you know where Mr. Emler is staying?" Nancy questioned.

"Maybe," Kiyabu replied. "Soon after his visit, Mr. Sakamaki grew very weak. He wrote two long letters. One was to young Mr. Sakamaki and the other to Mr. Emler. He asked me to mail them and I saw the addresses. Mr. Ralph Emler was visiting friends on Kapiolani Boulevard."

"Did this man come to Mr. Sakamaki's funeral?" the young sleuth inquired.

Kiyabu shook his head. "I never saw him again."

Nancy asked Kiyabu if he had any suggestions as to where she might start in trying to solve the mystery. He smiled. "I understand you are a famous girl detective. I am afraid poor Kiyabu could offer no help."

During the balance of the afternoon, Nancy walked round and round the Golden Pavilion, trying to figure out what its secret might be. There was no visible opening under the platform. Behind the latticework was concrete, studded with pieces of lava rock. Finally she gave up and went into the house. She made a tour of the mansion but nothing came to light which gave her any clue to the strange happenings.

"This mystery is going to be a real challenge," she told Ned, as they strolled outdoors after dinner.

Dusk had fallen and Nancy said she would like to watch the Golden Pavilion for a while to see if the dancing ghost Kiyabu had seen might appear. But though they watched the building from a vantage point among the trees for two hours, nothing happened.

In the morning, as Nancy was pondering over what new approach she could take in solving the mystery, Dave said, "Some of the other Emerson fellows have challenged us to an outrigger race. Are you all game?"

Bess was the first to answer. "I don't think our mixed group would stand a chance of winning. But if the rest of you want to try it, okay. Leave me out. You can have a crew of only five, anyway."

"You're both right and wrong," Dave told her. "We should have only five in the canoe, that's true, but we're going to win!"

Bess, Hannah, Emma, and Kiyabu said they would come down to the beach to watch the race and root for their friends. At ten o'clock the Emerson group of paddlers appeared offshore. Nancy and George climbed into the Kaluakua's outrigger canoe. Ned, Dave, and Burt followed, and each of them picked up a paddle. Ned sat in the stern to act as steersman.

The outrigger skimmed over the waves and soon was alongside the other canoe. Nancy and George knew four of the boys and were introduced to the fifth, who was the steersman. "Ready? Go!" he cried out.

The race was to be for half a mile along the beach to a buoy and back again. For a few minutes the two outriggers stayed side by side, then the one with the all-male crew began to pull ahead.

George scowled. "They mustn't beat us!" she called out. "Let's put on some steam!"

Everyone paddled harder, but they could not seem to catch up to their rivals. Finally Ned said, "I think our timing's off. We need better rhythm. When I call out, 'Dip—dip,' all pull together!"

As soon as he did, the paddling became smoother. The first canoe made the turn and started back. Soon Ned's group reached the half-mile mark and made a close turn, losing no time. Gradually the distance between the outriggers began to close.

Little by little, Ned urged his paddlers to dip faster. As the two canoes neared the finish line, George cried out that they must go even faster. With arms working so quickly that they were a blur to the watchers on shore, the mixed group of paddlers finally nosed alongside the other canoe. The race ended in a photo finish!

The hot, panting contestants lay their paddles across the canoes and caught their breaths. In a few moments, however, they were calling back and forth to one another.

"Didn't think you could do it!" said the steersman of the all-boy crew. "Congrats!"

The others laughed and Burt said, "All you need are girls who paddle like boys, and you're set!" Then he praised Nancy and George for their work.

The five Emerson boys waved good-by and started back for the Halekulani. Nancy and her friends picked up their paddles and turned toward shore. They had not gone far when Nancy, gazing at the Golden Pavilion, gave a start.

"Look!" she exclaimed. "A woman wearing a long white muumuu just crawled from underneath the pavilion!"

All eyes turned in the direction of the building. The woman was standing still and the watchers wondered if she were going to dance.

"But she couldn't have crawled from beneath the pavilion," George spoke up. "Kiyabu told me it has no opening."

Nancy nodded. "And I didn't find any. It must be well hidden."

Suddenly the woman started running toward the house. A moment later she disappeared among some shrubbery.

"Oh, she'll probably go inside!" Nancy cried out worriedly. "I'm sure the house is unlocked, and Bess and Hannah and Kiyabu and Emma aren't looking that way!"

She and George tried to signal the group on shore about what was happening, but none of them seemed to understand and stood awaiting the canoeists.

"I wonder if she's the 'ghost' Kiyabu saw," Nancy mused, "and why she's around in the daytime."

"The ghostly hula dancer!" Nancy exclaimed

The canoeists worked the paddles furiously as they came nearer and nearer the shore. Finally Dave and Burt jumped out and pulled the out-

rigger up onto the beach. With a quick explanation to those on shore, the others started running toward the house.

The woman in the long white muumuu was not in sight, but Nancy felt sure this meant she had already entered the house. "We'll surround the place, so that she can't escape!" the young sleuth suggested.

The others spread out, planning to encircle the building completely. Nancy and Ned dashed up the front porch and burst through the entrance into the hall.

At that moment, from somewhere inside the house, came a bloodcurdling scream!

CHAPTER XI

A Tantalizing Gift

As THE sounds of the scream faded, the watchers outside the house dashed in, some through the kitchen door, others through a side door to the sunroom. All ran to the front hall.

"Who was it?" Bess cried out. "And where is she?"

"We don't know, but everybody look for her!" Nancy ordered.

Part of the group bounded up the front stairway while Kiyabu and Emma took the rear one. Nancy, Ned, George, and Burt searched the rooms on the first floor. They looked in closets, behind curtains and screens, and even underneath pieces of furniture, but there was no sign of the woman in the white muumuu. Disappointed, the whole group of searchers met once more in the front hall.

"How could that woman have escaped from the

house?" Bess asked, puzzled. "We were watching every window and door."

"Up to a point, we were," Nancy replied. "But when the woman screamed, everyone who was outside came running in. It's my guess she grasped the opportunity to go out a window at that time."

"You mean," George spoke up, "that she screamed on purpose to lure us inside so she could get away?"

"Possibly," Nancy answered. "But also she may have been injured or frightened. I'm going to get my magnifying glass and see if I can find any clues."

She hurried upstairs and from one of her suitcases took the magnifying glass which her father had given her for Christmas. It was a very fine one and Nancy called it her "Pride and Joy."

When Nancy came downstairs again, Kiyabu followed her from place to place, his eyes lighting up with amazement as she made such amusing, but accurate remarks as: "Kiyabu, you really should ask Bess not to lean her elbows on the piano. It makes marks. And, Dave, when you dance, better not wear that tan sweater. It sheds."

Nancy's friends laughed and explained to Kiyabu that the young sleuth probably could have deduced this in the pitch dark. The caretaker shook his head in astonishment and remained silent. But he continued to follow Nancy around.

In the sunroom she stopped in front of a statue of a Japanese warrior. The figure was holding a samurai sword poised for action. Nancy examined the weapon carefully with her magnifying glass. Then she smiled.

"I believe the lady in the white muumuu screamed because she raked her head or arm on this sword."

"You mean there's blood on it?" Bess asked, horrified.

"No, but there are tiny bits of human flesh and hair."

Bess shivered as Ned stepped to the window near the statue. "And she probably went out here." He surveyed the flat, lava rock below.

Nancy nodded. The low, open window was well hidden by bushes, and the searchers were now convinced that the woman had escaped from the house this way. Since there were no fingerprints on the window sill, Nancy concluded that the woman had sat on it, whirled, and jumped down.

Nancy climbed out the window and Ned followed. With her magnifying glass, she examined the rocks carefully but could find no footprints. In the soft earth between a row of bushes, however, were small, light footprints.

"The woman doesn't weigh much," said Ned. "Right?"

"Right," Nancy agreed. "And she runs gracefully. She's probably a dancer. But all this doesn't help to identify her. Is she the wife of one of the Double Scorps? Or is she some other intruder mixed up with the mystery of Kaluakua?"

Directly after luncheon, Kiyabu announced two callers from Honolulu. One was a police detective, Sergeant Hawk, and the other an executor from the bank which was handling old Mr. Sakamaki's estate. He introduced himself as Henry Dutton. The men addressed most of their remarks to Nancy.

Sergeant Hawk spoke first. "Police Captain McGinnis of River Heights phoned Honolulu headquarters. He said your father had been in touch with him and suggested that someone from our department come to see you, Miss Drew. I understand that you have up-to-the-minute information on Mr. Sakamaki's case, and that certain suspicious things have happened since you became interested in Kaluakua."

Nancy gave a full account of all she knew in connection with the mystery, including the episode of the strange woman in the white muumuu. The detective, meanwhile, was busy making notes in a small book. From time to time he asked questions. Finally he put away his pencil and smiled at Nancy.

"This is a very fine, full report. The Honolulu police will start at once trying to locate the man who uses the names Jim O'Keefe and Tim O'Malley. From your description, we should have no trouble locating him. Also, we shall try to find Ralph Emler.

"As to the woman wearing the white muumuu, it's my deduction that she does not wear this except on occasions such as this morning. So it will be more difficult to locate her. Now I would like to examine the statue on which she scratched herself and also the footprints outside."

Ned offered to take the detective to the two spots, so that Nancy might talk further with Mr. Dutton.

"Would you mind telling me something about the claimants to the Sakamaki estate?" Nancy asked the banker.

"I'll be very happy to," Mr. Dutton replied. "In fact, after I was informed by the police about your prowess as a detective, Miss Drew, I decided to tell you everything and ask your assistance."

Nancy blushed a little. "Oh, I fail sometimes," she said modestly. "But I'll do everything I can to be of help."

Mr. Dutton told her that the two mysterious claimants to the Sakamaki fortune were very reticent. Roy Chatley and his sister Janet Lee had had little to say, apparently relying on the various papers they had with them to prove their case.

"Do they have a lawyer?" Nancy asked.

"Not yet," the executor replied. "But today they threatened to obtain one if we don't accept their credentials pretty soon."

"There's doubt in your mind, then, about them?" inquired Nancy.

"Naturally. I knew elderly Mr. Sakamaki well. It seems strange that he never mentioned the California relatives."

Mr. Dutton paused a moment, then said, "Since the estate is so large, it is certainly worth fighting for. So far the credentials of these California people seem to be in order, but I understand your father, Miss Drew, is going to stop in California on his way here and check everything."

Nancy asked if there were any letters from old Mr. Sakamaki to Janet and Roy or their mother or grandmother among the papers of proof.

"No," Mr. Dutton answered. "The brother and sister claim to have read a news account of the will in a California paper."

"Where are they staying?" Nancy inquired.

The executor replied that they were visiting friends named Pond in Honolulu. "I can't remember the address exactly. I'll send it to you," he promised.

By this time the police detective had finished his work. He returned to the house and a short while later the two men were saying *aloha* to Nancy and her friends. Both insisted that Nancy get in touch with them at once if any trouble developed at Kaluakua.

Just before a late dinner that evening, Kiyabu came into the sunroom where the guests were seated. He presented Nancy with a long box which evidently contained flowers. The caretaker waited as she opened it. Inside was a deep purple, almost black, sweet-smelling lei.

"How very unusual!" Nancy remarked, as she picked up the florist's envelope containing a card. Pulling it out, she read aloud, "From the Armstrongs."

"Why, isn't this sweet of them!" she exclaimed.

Nancy lifted the black lei from the box and started to put it around her neck. Seeing this, Kiyabu snatched it from her hands.

"Oh, please! No, no! Do not wear the lei!" he begged. "This is—this is a funeral offering!"

Nancy was mystified. Certainly the Armstrongs were familiar with the customs of the Islands. Why would they send her such a lei? Rising from her chair, she went at once to the telephone and called Mrs. Armstrong.

"A lei?" the woman repeated after Nancy. "Mr. Armstrong and I did not send it to you."

Nancy's heart skipped a beat and she stood lost in thought. Was the lei a threat from some unknown person?

CHAPTER XII

The Lei Maker's Hint

BEFORE rejoining the group in the living room, Nancy decided to call the florist where the lei apparently had been purchased.

Fortunately, the shop was still open. But upon looking at their records, the proprietor declared that he had not filled such an order.

"Is it true that a lei made of deep purple flowers is used as a funeral piece?" Nancy inquired.

The florist said that this was a custom among some people. He himself did not make such pieces, and he doubted that any florist would suggest one.

Nancy thanked the man for the information and put down the phone. More perplexed than ever, she returned to the group in the sunroom. "The lei didn't come from that florist," she told her friends. "It must have been made privately." Then she explained what she had learned.

George, curious to know more about the flowers, had picked up the lei and was examining it. "This is odd," she said suddenly. "Scattered here and there among the flowers are sharp-pointed, brownish-colored tacks."

As she pointed them out, Bess exclaimed, "And wherever the tacks are, the flowers are wilting!"

Nancy gazed at the mysterious lei. "Put it back in the box, George. I think those tacks have been dipped in poison."

"What!" Ned cried out, springing forward.

Nancy explained that she thought the sender had hoped she would wear the lei, be pricked, and poisoned.

"Oh, how horrible!" Bess exclaimed. "This mystery is getting to be dreadful."

Everyone was disturbed by the incident, and Ned remarked that the sender must indeed be desperate to resort to such measures. "But what I can't understand is why should he or she want to harm you personally?"

George answered for Nancy. "To get you away from here."

At this moment Hannah Gruen walked into the room. She had heard none of the conversation and everyone decided not to worry her. George quickly whisked the box of flowers behind her chair. The Drews' housekeeper did not notice her action. She announced that dinner was ready and requested that they come to the dining room.

Ned tarried behind and hid the box in the hall closet. He would bury the poisonous lei later, or give it to the police if they wanted it.

A delicious dinner was served by Kiyabu. It had been cooked by both Emma and Hannah who had become great culinary friends. Tonight the meal was strictly mainland—roast beef, with lemon meringue pie for dessert.

"If it's all right with you girls," Burt spoke up, "we fellows are going fishing in the outrigger canoe tomorrow morning."

"I wish you luck," George replied. "But you'd better bring in a big one to make amends for deserting us," she teased.

"Wow!" said Burt. "How can I fail?"

Nancy asked Ned if she might borrow the car to do some errands in Honolulu. She did not say what they were to be. In fact, she did not reveal what her main errand was until the following morning when she, Bess, and George were rolling along the highway.

"I'm determined to find out if possible who sent that floral piece," Nancy said. "Do you remember the section of road we passed on our way from the airport where a group of women were making and selling leis? I have a hunch the sender of my gift had a specialist make mine and it could be one of those women. Anyway, it won't hurt to ask them."

When she reached the area, the young sleuth

parked the car and the three girls began asking woman after woman if she had made a lei the day before of deep purple flowers. One after another answered no, until Nancy came to a very wrinkled old lady who was fashioning a beautiful lei of baby orchids. When Nancy put her question to the flower vendor, she looked up, startled.

"Why, yes, I did make such a lei yesterday afternoon. Why do you ask?"

Nancy searched the woman's face for any sign of dishonesty, but the wrinkled visage showed only genuine astonishment.

Nevertheless, Nancy decided that it was wiser not to tell the woman the whole truth. Pretending to giggle, she said that some unknown person had sent her the lei and she was trying to find out who he might be.

"An unknown admirer, eh?" the woman asked. Then she frowned. "To tell you the truth, I thought it was a funeral piece."

She went on to say that the man who had asked her to make it had brought the flowers himself. She described him as being tall, with reddish-blond hair. "I do not know his name," she added, "but I believe he is a mainlander."

"Did he ask you to put anything else in with the flowers?" Bess spoke up.

"No," the woman answered.

Nancy thanked her for the information, and the girls went back to the convertible.

"Reddish-blond hair!" said George. "That sounds like Ralph Emler, the same man we believe tricked Grandfather Sakamaki."

"Yes, it does," Nancy agreed. "And I think our next stop will be police headquarters. I hope Sergeant Hawk will be there. I want to tell him about the lei."

Fortunately, the officer was in. When the young sleuth told her story, the police detective looked concerned.

"I don't like this at all," he said. "Miss Drew, you must use extreme caution. So far we haven't been able to locate this Ralph Emler. We don't know whether he has left the city, is using an assumed name, or is staying in a private home. Emler left the place where he was staying, directly after receiving old Mr. Sakamaki's letter."

The girls talked for some time with the detective. Nancy asked him about the possibility of the California claimants to the Sakamaki estate being impostors. "It's possible, of course," the detective replied, "but so far we have found nothing suspicious about them or their credentials."

"I think I'll try to call on them," said Nancy. "May I use your phone, Sergeant Hawk?"

"Certainly." The detective pushed the instrument toward Nancy and gave her the number of the Ponds' residence. A rather petulant, flat voice answered the ring.

"Hel-lo."

"This is Nancy Drew calling. I should like very much to see Mrs. Lee and Mr. Chatley. Will you please find out if it would be all right for me to come to the house."

"Well, I dunno," the woman on the phone answered. "They don't see visitors much, but I'll ask 'em."

After a long wait, another woman's voice said hello. "This is Mrs. Lee speaking. You wish to see me?" she asked.

Nancy repeated her request. There was a long pause as if Janet Lee was consulting someone else. Then she said, "Why, certainly. I'd love to have you. When do you want to come?"

"Right away," Nancy replied. "And I'd like to bring two friends who are in town with me."

"Come ahead," Janet Lee invited. "I'll be waiting for you."

On the way to the Ponds' residence, Bess declared that she was not going inside the house. She even begged Nancy to hold the conference in their garden. "After that black lei episode, I trust hardly anybody around here," she declared.

Nancy laughed. "All right. I only hope the Ponds have a garden."

Bess's wish was gratified. The house was set some distance from the street and was surrounded by a high hedge. A driveway led to the front door through a most attractive garden.

Bess and George seated themselves in lawn

chairs, while Nancy rang the front doorbell. It was opened by a middle-aged woman wearing a long, dark-blue muumuu. Her blond hair was rather frizzy and unkempt.

"Mrs. Lee?" Nancy asked.

"Oh my, no. I'm Mrs. Pond. Janet'll be here in a minute. She's gettin' prettied up for you folks."

Nancy took an instant dislike to Mrs. Pond. When the woman invited her inside, she said, "Oh, it's so lovely out in the garden, I'd prefer staying outside."

Mrs. Pond shrugged. "Have it your own way."

At that moment Janet Lee and Roy Chatley appeared. The brother and sister did not look at all alike. He was taller than she and had light hair and a pale complexion. His sister was small and slight with dark hair and a sallow complexion. At Nancy's suggestion they joined Bess and George in the garden.

"Why have you come here?" Janet asked abruptly.

Nancy was slightly taken aback, but she kept her composure and said, "I am a friend of Mr. Sakamaki in River Heights. In fact, my father is his lawyer. I understand you are distantly related to him."

"Yes," Roy replied in a soft tone, "We had the same grandfather, although I understand the Mr. Sakamaki you know was never told this." Suddenly Roy said in a loud, unpleasant voice, "It was pretty mean the way Grandfather treated his first wife. Oh, well, we can forgive a lot if we just get the inheritance. Boy, what I couldn't do with that money!"

Nancy and her friends were disgusted with Roy's approach to the subject. They learned little that they did not already know, and presently said good-by.

"They're just horrid," Bess remarked as Nancy drove off.

Soon after reaching the highway, Nancy stopped, pulled to the side of the road, and said, "I think my next bit of sleuthing will be talks with the neighbors of the Ponds, and finding out what I can about that couple. They just don't seem like the kind of people one would expect to live in this fine residential area."

CHAPTER XIII

A Valuable Discovery

THE GIRLS found most of the Ponds' neighbors in their gardens. Nancy, Bess, and George discreetly inquired of one after another if they were acquainted with the couple. In each case the answer was the same. The Ponds had rented the house very recently and no one knew them. They appeared to be unsociable and were away from the house a great deal.

"Are they Hawaiians?" Nancy asked an elderly man.

"Oh, I think not. I'm sure that they are from the mainland," he replied.

When the girls returned to the car, one of the women to whom she had spoken earlier was waiting for them. Nancy wondered if she had further information, but the woman merely smiled and asked if the girls were going into Honolulu. Upon learning that they were, she asked for a lift, explaining that her husband was using their car that day for a business trip.

"We'd be happy to take you," Nancy said, and they all got in.

On the way, the passenger, whose name was Mrs. Ayers, pointed out a thickly branched tree with dense foliage. "That is a monkeypod," she said. "Many of them grow on the island of Kauai, and the wood is brought here to be made into attractive pieces. I'm going to a shop now that specializes in these pieces to buy a wedding gift."

"The tree certainly looks top heavy," Bess remarked. "Its long limbs seem to be way out of proportion with the size of the trunk."

"Is the wood hard?" George asked.

"Yes," Mrs. Ayers answered. "It's very durable, and won't warp or crack."

"I'd like to look at some of the wooden pieces," Nancy remarked. "We want to take home some gifts and this is a good chance to purchase them."

When they reached the Waikiki Beach section, Mrs. Ayers told Nancy where to park and the four walked to the shop. After looking over the many attractive articles on display, George selected a snack server, Bess a tray, and Nancy a salad bowl with wooden fork and spoon.

"Not far from here," Mrs. Ayers told the girls, "is an extremely interesting jewelry shop. It specializes in ivory pieces. If you have time, I'd suggest you drop in there."

She went to the door with the girls and pointed out the shop. With a "thank you so much" and an "aloha" to Mrs. Ayers, the three hurried up the street and entered the jewelry store.

The display case intrigued the girls. Ivory pins, earrings, necklaces, and bracelets were delicately carved in patterns of various Hawaiian flowers.

"I see just the right gift for Aunt Eloise," said Nancy, and asked the clerk the price of a pin and earring set carved in the ginger flower design.

"Will you mail this directly to New York?" Nancy inquired.

"I'd be very glad to," the clerk replied.

After the sale was completed, the girls returned to the convertible, and this time headed straight for Kaluakua. As they parked in the driveway, Ned greeted them with a friendly gibe.

"For Pete's sake, where have you been? Here we boys speared the biggest fish of the season and we've waited and waited hours for you to come home and admire it."

The girls laughed. "What is it and where is it?" George asked.

"It's an ulua," said Ned, "and what a time we had capturing the old boy. He was a real fighter and towed our outrigger along as if it were a feather."

Only Bess was impressed. Nancy and George were sure the story was grossly exaggerated.

Grinning, Nancy said, "Come on, Ned, tell us the truth. How big is this fish?"

"Follow me," Ned suggested, and they all trooped to the kitchen.

The ulua, minus its head, tail, and fins, lay on the kitchen table and the girls had to admit that it was a good-sized fish.

"We may as well tell you the truth," Dave spoke up. "Hero Ned speared this fish all by himself under water. But I guess it wasn't too much of a battle."

Ned grinningly admitted that it had not been too hard to spear the fish. "We're going to have it for lunch," he stated. "So we'd all better go for a swim and work up an appetite."

Hannah Gruen smiled. "But not too big an appetite," she said. "Mr. and Mrs. Armstrong telephoned and they're going to serve a native feast tonight—a *luau*."

"How exciting!" spoke up Bess, who was always ready to eat.

The Drews' housekeeper went on to say that the Armstrongs had invited the mainlanders to come to their home for the feast. But Hannah had told them that Nancy and the others probably would not want to be away from Kaluakua for so many hours because of the mystery.

"So the Armstrongs offered to come here and prepare the feast," she announced. "Kiyabu says there is a pit in the garden where pigs were roasted for luaus years ago.   "He's going to fix it up and heat the lava rock which is put into the pit. The pig has to be steamed."

"Mm-m! I can't wait," Bess remarked, and began to lick her lips in anticipation of the feast.

As Nancy glanced toward Ned, she detected a slightly hurt expression on his face.

"It won't taste any better than this fish," she said quickly.

The young man beamed at her, then said, "Nancy, the undersea life offshore here is fascinating.   I dare you to go skin diving with me to see it."

"I'll do it!" Nancy agreed.   "Tomorrow!"

"It's a date."

Everyone enjoyed the ulua at lunch.   Directly afterward, Nancy suggested that the whole group go on an exhaustive search of the premises to try learning what Grandfather Sakamaki's secret might be.   Walls were tapped for hollow spaces. Floors and ceilings were inspected for trap doors. Nothing came to light.

Finally Bess, heaving a great sigh, remarked, "I'm afraid that Grandpa Sakamaki was just spoofing.   He just didn't want this estate to go out of the hands of the family, so he made up the whole thing."

The group was in the living room.   George had crawled beneath a heavy teakwood table and was tapping the underside. Suddenly the others heard her give a squeal of amazement.

"I've found a hidden drawer!" she exclaimed.

At once the other young people were down on hands and knees and crowding close to her under the table.

"There's a panel that slides. It must be a secret drawer. Yes, here it is and there are some things in it!" George cried out gleefully.

Burt helped her lift out the hidden drawer which was filled with small, dark wooden statuettes. One by one the objects were set on the table.

"What a find!" said Ned enthusiastically. "I'll bet these are ancient and valuable."

When Kiyabu was summoned he gazed in awe and amazement at the figurines. He had never seen them before. He, too, thought they were old and that Mr. Sakamaki Sr. would never have taken the trouble to hide them unless they were valuable.

"I know Mr. Uni at the museum," he said. "Maybe he would come up here to look at them."

Nancy thought this a good idea and asked Kiyabu to put in the call to Mr. Uni. In a little while the Polynesian expert arrived. The small, bright-eyed curator examined each piece carefully. Finally, he declared that the statuettes were very old and authentic but not ancient.

"The museum would like very much to have

these," Mr. Uni said. "Perhaps the estate would sell or donate them to us later. In the meantime, I believe they would be much safer locked up down there than they would be here. I understand there have been some strange happenings at Kaluakua."

"Yes," Kiyabu answered. "One can never seem to tell when there may be prying eyes. Now that these pieces have been found, I think they should be taken away and put into a safe."

Nancy offered to call Mr. Dutton and ask his advice in the matter. When the executor learned of the discovery, he agreed that the museum was the place for the statuettes.

"Miss Drew, will you please write out a receipt with full description of each piece and ask Mr. Uni to sign it," he requested. "Also I'd appreciate it if you'd send someone to the bank with it."

"I'll be very happy to," Nancy replied. "I'll ask the boys to accompany Mr. Uni to the museum, then deliver the receipt to you."

"Very good," said Mr. Dutton.

Kiyabu supplied paper and pen, and Nancy wrote down a detailed account of each object. Most of the statuettes represented ancient gods of the Polynesians, but others were of former Hawaiian kings.

After the boys had left with Mr. Uni, Kiyabu went back to the garden where he had been cleaning out the old fire pit in which the pig for the feast would be roasted. Near it, he had built a raging bonfire in a depression of the garden.

On the ground stood a bucket of water. Every once in a while Kiyabu would lift a sample rock from the fire in a huge pair of tongs and drop it into the water, apparently to test the intensity of the heat.

Hannah said that she was going out to the garden to sit in the shade near the picnic spot and rest. She invited the girls to join her when they finished searching.

"I think we should quit work now," Bess stated. "If we don't, we'll all be worn out for the party tonight."

Nancy was reluctant to leave her job unfinished. But she realized that since arriving at Kaluakua she had not spent much time with Hannah, so she decided to follow her to the garden. The group of four seated themselves in comfortable chairs, their backs to the area where the fire was burning.

Kiyabu left his task and walked to the house. Reaching the porch he turned to look back and stood transfixed with horror.

A furtive figure had appeared from the bushes. Quick as a flash, the man had grabbed up the huge fire tongs lying on the ground and was about to heave them toward Nancy!

CHAPTER XIV

Meeting a Shark

"Auwe! Wikiwiki!" Kiyabu screamed from the porch of the house. Nancy and the others did not know what he meant, but instinctively they turned in the direction he was facing.

Nancy was not a moment too soon. The heavy tongs were coming straight at her. Like a flash, she leaped aside just as the tongs buried themselves in a nearby bush.

"Mercy!" Bess exclaimed, clutching her heart.

George, who had seen the man near the fire, called out, "There goes the fellow who threw them!"

In an instant she was dashing across the grass after him. Nancy and Bess followed. The fleeing man dodged in and out among the trees and shrubbery until he reached the entrance to Kaluakua. By the time the girls arrived at the spot, he was a good distance down the road. A small black car which had been parked in the bushes picked him up and sped off.

The angry girls stood still, staring after it. The automobile was too far away for them to read the license plate.

"One of the Scorps, I'll bet," George found her voice. "Thank goodness Kiyabu saw him and warned you, Nancy."

"Yes," Bess added. "Why, Nancy, you might have been killed by those heavy tongs."

Nancy was silent. She was a bit shaken by the experience, and was puzzled as to who the man might be. He was of medium height and had thinning, dark hair.

"I wonder if he's Jim O'Keefe, alias Tim O'Malley," she mused.

The girls returned to the picnic spot to find Hannah and Kiyabu extremely upset. Nancy tried to soothe them, while George asked what the caretaker had called out.

"'Auwe' means 'alas!' Woe is me! And 'wiki wiki,' you were to 'hurry.' Oh, I am so glad you did."

"Thank you for the warning, Kiyabu," Nancy said solemnly, then added that she was going to report the matter to the police at once.

Sergeant Hawk was greatly concerned upon learning what had happened. He did not mention sending anyone to guard the place, however, and Nancy did not bring up the subject. The detective seemed to be in a hurry to report the matter and try to have the getaway car apprehended.

Soon after Nancy returned to the garden, the three boys arrived. All were wearing very gay Aloha shirts which they said they had purchased in the city after delivering the receipt to Mr. Dutton.

"These shirts are in honor of the luau," Dave announced.

"I suppose we should be wearing muumuus or hula costumes," Nancy reflected aloud.

Hannah smiled. "I have a surprise for you girls," she said. "Come upstairs."

Nancy and her chums followed Hannah Gruen to the second floor. There she handed each of the girls a muumuu—a white one for Nancy, a blue for Bess, and a pale green for George.

"How lovely!" said Nancy. "Where did these come from?"

"Emma sent them over," the housekeeper revealed. "She thought you might want to wear them tonight."

"How very sweet of her!" said Bess.

The girls put on the muumuus and went to thank Emma. Then they joined the boys and told them about the vicious tongs thrower.

"I'm going to stick around after this, so I can take care of you!" Ned declared, and Nancy smiled appreciatively.

A short time later Mr. and Mrs. Armstrong and their Polynesian maid arrived with the food for the Hawaiian feast and leis for the mainlanders.

"May we help with the luau?" Nancy asked.

"Yes," she said. "I think you girls would enjoy setting the table."

"But first," Mr. Armstrong spoke up, "I think our guests should watch the preparation of the pig."

Kiyabu produced a huge piece of chicken wire which was then covered with banana leaves. The pig was laid on them. Next, he picked up one of the hot lava stones with the tongs and placed it inside the animal. Then sweet potatoes and pieces of fish which had been wrapped in ti leaves were placed around the pig.

Slowly the wire tray, with its luscious load, was lowered into the pit lined with the hot lava rocks. More banana leaves were spread over it, then large wet sacks. Finally, dirt was heaped on the top.

"This is called the *imu,* or oven," Mrs. Armstrong explained. "The pig cooked in the imu is called *puaa kalua* and will be left for four hours to steam."

While waiting for the food to cook, the young people told Mr. and Mrs. Armstrong about the recent mysterious happenings. Next, they took them on a tour of the house and showed them the table where the valuable old statuettes had been found. They all did some further searching, but nothing came of it.

"Let's gather flowers for the luau now," Mrs. Armstrong suggested.

She and the girls walked around the extensive grounds, gathering red, orange, pink, yellow, and purple hibiscus flowers. Next, long tapa mats were brought from the Armstrong car and spread on the ground, not far from the roasting pig.

Their hostess had also brought a basket of ti leaves and she now sprinkled them on the mats. Among these, the girls dropped the hibiscus blossoms.

Presently Emma appeared with luscious-looking pineapples and bananas which were interspersed with the flowers. "I never saw a prettier table decoration," Bess murmured.

At each place the Armstrongs set a coconut shell filled with *poi*. Bess gazed at the sticky, pastelike porridge, which she was told was made from the root of the taro plant, and wondered if she dared to eat it.

Mr. Armstrong was amused. "Poi is rather flavorless, but you should at least taste it," he urged.

Meanwhile, the Armstrongs' maid was busy in the kitchen, grinding coconut and pounding squid. This fish would be roasted brown with sea salt and served with crushed *kukui* nuts.

Emma was filling coconut shell dishes with salmon and onion and tomatoes. Dessert, she said, would be white squares of delicious coconut pudding.

By the time the pig was ready to eat, dusk had fallen. Mr. Armstrong stuck several kukui-nut torches into the ground and lighted them. As the young people gathered around the table with the others, Mrs. Armstrong smiled broadly.

"You really look like Hawaiians," she said. "Now, everyone find his place, please."

Her guests discovered that place cards had been set among the flowers and leaves.

"Why, our names are in Hawaiian!" Bess exclaimed. "Oh, dear, how can I ever find mine?"

Nancy was the first to discover hers. She declared it was not too hard to figure out. "Ane is a little like my American name," she said, smiling.

Hannah was next to find her name. It was Ana Palani. "I presume that stands for Hannah Frances," she said, turning to Mrs. Armstrong. "I wondered why you asked me earlier what my middle name was."

The other young people found it impossible to figure out their cards. Finally their hostess led them one by one to their places. Bess's Hawaiian name was Elikapeka. George's was Keoki. "Yours, Ned," said Mrs. Armstrong, "is Eluwene."

Eluwene was glad to be seated next to Nancy. Burt, called Topaka, was next to George, and

Kawiki, meaning, 'Dave,' was placed next to Bess.

"Oh, this is such fun!" Nancy exclaimed. To herself she added, "And I hope nothing happens tonight to mar this beautiful party!"

Everyone seated himself on the ground at the luau table and Mr. Armstrong proudly carried the crisply brown steamed pig to the table on a wooden platter.

"Kiyabu was going to do this," he said, "but he has elected himself a guard of the grounds tonight."

The feast was pronounced by everyone to be most delicious—and filling. While the group was eating dessert, they suddenly heard the soft strains of a guitar. Looking up, they saw a man in a gay yellow-and-brown satin suit walking toward them. Four hula dancers followed him.

"A little surprise we planned for you," Mrs. Armstrong told her guests.

"How absolutely divine!" Bess burst out.

The guitarist bowed and smiled, then began to sing. The four dancers started to sway in time to the music, moving a few steps to left and right, and gracefully raising their arms.

"This is a dance welcoming you to the Islands," Mrs. Armstrong told the mainlanders.

All too soon the party ended with the mainlanders declaring that they had never had a more festive meal nor a more enjoyable evening.

"And so romantic!" Bess declared dreamily. "Oh, I just love this place!"

Nancy was happy that her chum apparently had forgotten her fears about dangerous happenings at Kaluakua. Before going to bed, she and Ned took a stroll around the grounds and spoke to Kiyabu. The caretaker insisted that he was going to stay up all night to patrol the estate.

"How about me spelling you?" Ned offered, but Kiyabu refused.

At breakfast the next morning the caretaker reported that there had been no disturbance during the night, and he hoped that all intruders had now been discouraged.

"Ane, are you ready to do some skin diving?" Ned asked an hour later, his eyes twinkling. "Eluwene awaits you."

Chuckling, Nancy went upstairs, put on her bathing suit, then joined Ned on the beach. After he had adjusted a transparent helmet over her head and strapped an oxygen tank on her back, Nancy slipped her feet into flippers.

Then Ned donned his equipment and the two walked into the surf. Upon reaching deeper water, they both swam downward.

"How fascinating this is!" Nancy said to herself, as myriads of small fish of various colors swam past her.

The couple presently came to a cave and

paused to watch a small octopus-type creature waving its tentacles about the opening. Nancy was so intent on its maneuvers to collect food by reaching out at passing small prey that she did not notice a very large fish swimming toward her.

As she turned to swim off she was struck with horror. The huge fish, its jaws wide open, was only a few feet away. A man-eating shark, she thought!

Ned, who had become aware of the shark at almost the same moment, gave Nancy a tremendous push upwards. Then he followed her. The two twisted and turned to get out of danger, diving and rising until they eluded the shark and came to the surface. They raced toward shore, constantly looking back over their shoulders to see if they were being followed.

Exhausted and their hearts pounding, the two finally reached the beach. As they dropped down, panting, and telling each other what a narrow escape they had had, Kiyabu came walking toward them. A short distance behind him were Burt, George, Bess, and Dave. When they had all gathered around, Nancy and Ned told them about their harrowing experience.

Kiyabu all the while was looking off over the water. At last he said, "I do not wish to take away anything from your bravery, but in the waters of the Hawaiian Islands there are no man-eating sharks. They are all harmless."

The shark was only a few feet away

"Boy, do I feel silly!" Ned exclaimed. "Well, live and learn!"

Kiyabu said with a twinkle in his eyes, "Don't you remember? Kaahupahau, the Queen of the Sharks, keeps the man-eaters away?"

George now spoke up. "There may not be any man-eating sharks around here, but there are some human sharks."

She related that a man whom Kiyabu and Emma had never seen before had come to the estate right after Nancy left. He had said that Mr. Dutton had sent him because he was a dealer in antiques and was willing to buy some of the valuable objects.

"But the sums he offered for them were perfectly ridiculous," George reported.

Burt declared that he was sure the man was not a dealer at all. "I think he was just a snooper, probably one of the Double Scorps."

Nancy was disturbed by the information. Jumping up, she declared, "I've been playing long enough. I must get back to work on the mystery at once!"

Bess's face broke into a broad grin. "Nancy, while you were gone, Dave and I did some sleuthing," she announced proudly. "Wait until you hear what we found out!"

CHAPTER XV

The Silversword's Secret

AFTER Nancy had showered and put on a sports dress, the young people gathered in the garden and Bess began her story.

"We decided to try surprising you," she said. "Dave and I kept thinking about that woman who seemed to come from underneath the pavilion. So we decided to look for a secret opening."

"And we found one!" Dave told the young sleuth. "I feel now as though I really belong on your detective team, Nancy!"

"There's a cunningly concealed door in the foundation," Bess continued. "It swings inward on a hinge. The door was left slightly ajar."

Nancy was thrilled. "Did you find anything underneath the pavilion?"

"Yes, we did," Dave replied. "There's a three-foot space between the ground and the floor of the pavilion. I began digging in the dirt and this is what I came up with."

The young man reached behind a nearby bush and brought out a small metal chest. He opened the lid and took out a piece of paper on which were a drawing and two identical symbols that looked a little like men. They were joined at the base.

Nancy stared at them. "Why, this a sketch of a silversword plant!" she exclaimed. "The only place in the world that it grows is in the Haleakala Crater over on the island of Maui."

"You're practically right," Burt spoke up. "There also are some silversword plants in desolate sections of the island of Hawaii."

"Anyway, it's a marvelous clue, I'm sure," said Nancy. "Did you find out what these symbols mean?" she asked excitedly.

George grinned. "The translation is my contribution to this clue," she said. "The symbol is *na kanata* and that's Polynesian for men. I asked Kiyabu and he found an old book with ancient symbols of the Pacific islands."

Nancy was delighted with the additional find. "This is simply wonderful. Thanks a million!"

When Bess asked what the next move would be,

Nancy said, "I think we should go to Haleakala Crater and try to find out if this clue was Grandfather Sakamaki's method of giving directions to whatever treasure he secreted."

"You mean," George spoke up, *"Kupunakane Sakamaki."* She chuckled. "That is Grandfather in Hawaiian."

Nancy laughed. "George, you've certainly been busy. All right, this is a clue, I'm sure, to Kupunakane Sakamaki's secret."

"You mean, it's a summons to the crater?" Bess asked and Nancy nodded.

Ned had said little up to this time. Now he voiced the opinion that possibly the woman in the white muumuu who had crawled from beneath the Golden Pavilion had buried the chest and it was not connected with the secret at all.

"But why would she do such a thing?" Bess asked.

"To draw Nancy Drew away from Kaluakua," Ned replied.

"If that was her reason," George spoke up, "surely she wouldn't put it in such an obscure place."

"Remember, she left the door ajar," Nancy said.

The young people talked at length about the two ideas regarding the silversword plant and the symbols under it which meant men. Finally they appealed to Kiyabu for an opinion.

"I am sure Mr. Sakamaki Sr. put the chest there

himself," the Hawaiian replied. "He was a man who was very learned and also full of fun. I believe he enjoyed scattering the pieces of the puzzle for his grandson to put together."

"That convinces me," Nancy declared. "I'm going to Haleakala Crater. Who wants to come along?"

Everyone wanted to make the trip, including Hannah Gruen. Kiyabu offered to make the hotel and plane reservations, and telephone to Maui for a guide with a car to take them to the crater.

"This guide knows the mountains and the history of the volcanoes well," Kiyabu said. "If anyone on the island can help you solve the mystery, I am sure he can. His name is Moki Kuano, but just call him Moki."

A little later the caretaker informed the group that he had secured reservations for the following day on the afternoon plane. This meant they would be able to see the gorgeous sunset over the crater.

Luncheon was served in the garden. Nancy and her friends had just finished eating, when Kiyabu brought her a message. "The telegraph office phoned that your father will arrive by plane tomorrow morning. Would you like me to meet him?"

"Thank you very much," Nancy replied, "but I'd love to meet Dad myself."

Ned offered to go with Nancy to the airport. They left Kaluakua before breakfast the next morning, deciding to get a snack at the field while waiting for Mr. Drew.

The great plane was on time, and the couple watched as it circled the field and landed smoothly. Nancy had purchased a lei of bright red plumiera blossoms and stood at the fence eagerly awaiting her father.

The passengers began to disembark. As each one appeared in the doorway of the plane, Nancy looked hopefully for Mr. Drew. Finally the pilot, the copilot, steward, and stewardess alighted. It was evident that there was no one else aboard.

"Dad didn't come!" Nancy exclaimed to Ned. "Oh, I hope nothing has happened to him!"

Ned was worried too, but said cheerfully, "Perhaps there is a message at the airlines office, or possibly your father sent another telegram."

He and Nancy hurried inside the building and made inquiries, but there was no word from Mr. Drew. Nancy telephoned to Kaluakua and asked if anyone there had heard from her father. The answer was no.

Going to the airlines' reservation desk, Nancy asked, "Could you find out if my father, Mr. Drew, made the reservation and then canceled it?"

The clerk made two telephone calls, then said that the lawyer had first canceled, then reinstated his reservation. "But Mr. Drew never claimed the ticket," he added, "so it was sold to someone else at the last minute."

"That's not like Dad," Nancy said worriedly to Ned as they walked away. "I'm going to telephone Mr. Sakamaki in River Heights and see if he knows why Dad wasn't on the plane."

She put in the long-distance call from the airport, and fortunately Mr. Sakamaki himself answered. When he heard Nancy's story, he was astounded. "I haven't heard of any change in your father's plans," he said. "But I believe I can help you find out what happened. I'll phone a private detective I know in Los Angeles and ask him to work on the case. As soon as I learn anything, I'll let you know."

"Oh, please do," Nancy begged. "I'm going directly to Kaluakua now and I'll wait there until I hear from you."

She and Ned hurried back to the estate. The first person they met was Hannah, who became greatly alarmed upon hearing that Mr. Drew had not arrived in Honolulu. "He's probably being detained by some of those Double Scorps," she fretted.

She and the others were relieved to know that a detective was going to start work immediately to find out what had happened. Despite this, a feeling of gloom settled over Kaluakua and all the mainlanders sat around talking in low tones.

"Do you think we should cancel our reservations to Maui?" Ned asked Nancy, as noon approached.

"Let's wait until one o'clock," she suggested.

At that moment the telephone rang and she quickly picked up the receiver. The others had risen from their chairs and, with worried expressions, tiptoed forward. They were thunderstruck to hear Nancy cry out, "Dad!"

There was a long, one-sided conversation. Finally the young sleuth said good-by to her father and turned to the others.

"That Los Angeles detective is a whiz," she remarked. "He found Dad very quickly, although he had moved to another hotel. And he also learned that there was an impostor, one of the Double Scorps, using the name of Carson Drew. This man passed himself off as Dad and canceled the cable to me saying my father's trip had been delayed. He also reinstated the plane reservation, which Dad had canceled. Of course Dad never showed up to pay for it, so the fellow bought it at the last moment at the airport to use himself."

"Well, thank goodness Mr. Drew is all right," Hannah spoke up. "Is he remaining in Los Angeles?"

"He said he'd see us after we get back from the volcano country," Nancy answered.

As she finished speaking, she heard a car coming up the driveway. Curious about the newcomer, everyone trooped to the front porch to see who was coming.

"Why, it's Janet Lee and Roy Chatley!" Bess said in a low tone.

"I wonder what they want," George mused, frowning.

The brother and sister jumped from the car. They gave fleeting smiles to the mainlanders, then opened the luggage compartment of the automobile. From it, Roy began taking out several suitcases. Presently, he picked up two of the bags and carried them to the porch. Turning to Ned, he said:

"Give me a hand with the rest of the luggage, will you?"

Nancy had stepped forward. "We—we're glad to see you, but why the luggage?"

By this time Janet was walking up the front steps. "We've come to stay," she announced.

Looks of astonishment came over the faces of Nancy and her friends. The young detective managed to say, "You're staying? Mr. Sakamaki has invited you to come here?"

"Of course not," Janet Lee answered. "But as to an invitation, Roy and I don't need one. We have far more right to be here than you people have. We're staying!"

"Furthermore," her brother added pompously, "the sooner you folks move out, the better we'll like it!"

CHAPTER XVI

The Specter

COMPLETELY stunned by the announcement of Roy Chatley and Janet Lee, Nancy's group stood as if rooted to the spot. They could not believe what they had just heard. The brother and sister were moving in and asking the others to move out!

"Well, aren't you fellows going to help me with the bags?" Roy asked in an irritable voice.

As Nancy found her voice and introduced Mrs. Gruen and the boys, Ned stepped forward and said, "As soon as I'm told it's all right, I'll be glad to help you with your luggage."

Janet tossed her head. "Well, of all the nerve! Here we're the grandchildren of the man who owned this place and you're telling us what to do."

By now Nancy had decided what to do. She hurried into the house and dashed upstairs to Grandfather Sakamaki's bedroom. Adjoining it was a small study with a telephone. She closed the door and put in a call to Mr. Dutton, the executor.

When Nancy related what had happened, the trust officer was stunned by the news. "This makes a complicated situation indeed," he said. "But I suppose we have no right to keep Mrs. Lee and her brother out. They are entitled to visit the estate as well as your friend Mr. Sakamaki or any friends he sends there."

"I suppose so," Nancy agreed. "I only hope they'll be pleasant."

Mr. Dutton sighed. "I wish I could help you, but at the moment nothing occurs to me. Just this morning I was going over the credentials of Mrs. Lee and Mr. Chatley. They certainly seem to be all right.

"Among the things is a photograph of the grave of old Mr. Sakamaki's first wife, their grand-mother. Then they had other papers to prove that she had just one child, a daughter. The photograph of this woman proved that she looked very much like her mother.

"Then there were other old photographs of Mr. Sakamaki's first wife with her grandchildren. They certainly resemble Janet and Roy. Also, they produced newspaper clippings of the death notice and funeral of their mother."

Nancy was impressed. "It all sounds authentic," she said.

"Yes, it does," Mr. Dutton agreed. "Another

thing, Mr. Chatley brought an old letter of his grandmother's to a friend telling how her husband had left her when their daughter was a baby and that he had gone to Honolulu."

"It sounds very plausible," Nancy had to admit. "Mr. Dutton, as you know, my father is in Los Angeles trying to check the same story. I talked with him on the phone this morning and he said something had come up which had made him decide to stay over and do some further investigating. Maybe he'll uncover additional facts that will disprove Roy's claim."

Nancy then told of the proposed trip to Maui and the Haleakala Crater. She explained about the little metal chest and the pictures on the paper found inside.

"How interesting!" the executor remarked.

"It may or may not mean anything," said Nancy, "but I suspect it's a good clue to the mystery of Kaluakua. "I'd planned to fly today to the area where the silversword plants are, but I hate to go and leave Roy Chatley and his sister here."

"I see," said Mr. Dutton. "Well, go ahead. I'll have a private detective, named John Jerral, come out to the house and stay while you're away."

Nancy was relieved. "That's fine, Mr. Dutton." With a chuckle, she added, "I don't think we should tell Janet and Roy what his profession is."

"Right," the executor agreed. "Mr. Jerral is

of medium height and a bit overweight. "I'll ask him to wear a green necktie, so that you'll recognize him. Good-by, Miss Drew, and success on your search."

Crossing the study, Nancy opened the door, walked through Mr. Sakamaki's bedroom, and into the hall. There she met Janet Lee and her brother. The young woman held two small suitcases, her brother two large ones. At this instant they plunked them down on the floor.

"Roy," said Janet, "I'm going to look over all the rooms, then decide which ones you and I will occupy."

"Most of them are taken," Nancy spoke up. "Suppose I show you two that are empty."

"Thank you, but I'll make my own decision," retorted Janet haughtily. "Since this house belongs partly to me, I think I have a right to sleep where I want to."

Nancy did not argue with the woman. She and her friends would be leaving that afternoon and not returning for a while. Perhaps by the time they came back to Kaluakua, Mr. Drew would be there and she could get his advice in the matter.

Casually, Nancy said that she and her friends and Mrs. Gruen were making a trip to Maui to see the famous crater. When they returned, the group could discuss the matter of who should stay at the estate. Janet's and Roy's faces lighted up, but their smiles faded when Nancy said:

"Kaluakua is to have another guest for a short time. He will arrive soon. His name is Mr. John Jerral. He's a very pleasant man, and I'm sure you'll enjoy his company."

"What does he do?" Roy Chatley asked suspiciously.

"Oh, he's interested in many things," Nancy replied noncommittally. "He's really a very well-informed person. "He'll be able to tell you a lot about the Hawaiian Islands and their legends and history."

Leaving it to Mr. Jerral to satisfy Roy's curiosity, Nancy rushed downstairs. She quickly told the others of her conversation with the executor and the fact that Mr. Jerral was coming. "But I didn't tell Janet and Roy what his profession is."

Bess laughed. "And we shan't give it away. I'll go tell Kiyabu and Emma about it." She hurried away.

George said in a giggling whisper that she had better go and rescue her purse from the bedroom before Roy decided it belonged to the estate! Everyone went upstairs and watched the newcomers choose their bedrooms.

First Ned's suitcase and clothes were rudely removed from his room by Roy. Nancy was dismayed because this was one of the most spacious rooms on the second floor and she had planned that Mr. Drew would sleep in the room with Ned.

"I think I'll take this room," Janet announced

in grandiose style, as she stopped in the doorway of the room which Nancy was sharing with Hannah. "I'd appreciate it if whoever is in here would remove these clothes."

Nancy concealed her annoyance and said nothing. Bess and George helped her carry the clothes to a small room at the end of the hall.

As George hung up the last dress, she said with flashing eyes, "Do you girls realize that those two have picked rooms from which they can watch everything that goes on?"

"Yes, and everybody!" added Bess. "It wouldn't surprise me if by the time we get back here all the clothes we've left have been stolen!"

"Oh, I don't think we need worry about that," said Nancy. She glanced at her watch. "We'd better grab some lunch and be on our way or we'll miss our plane."

Soon she and her friends were ready to leave. Suitcases were piled into the convertible's luggage compartment and its passengers began to climb in. Nancy was worried. Mr. Jerral had not arrived and she had great misgivings about leaving Janet Lee and Roy Chatley at Kaluakua without more professional guards than Kiyabu and Emma.

But a moment later her fears were allayed. A car turned into the driveway, and a slightly stout man of medium build and wearing a green necktie parked and stepped out. Nancy rushed forward and told him in a low voice what had happened, including the fact that Janet Lee and Roy Chatley did not know that he was a detective.

"Good!" he said in a whisper. Aloud he called, "You'll love the island of Maui. Have a fine time!"

An hour later the group were in the air. Nancy and Ned sat together and soon were discussing the various aspects of the mystery.

"Tell me your idea of what the *na kanata* symbol may mean, Ned," Nancy said.

"My guess is statuettes," he replied. "Perhaps there are two very valuable statuettes buried near some silversword plant."

Nancy gazed out the window at the greenish-blue water below her as she thought about this. Then she reflected that a silversword plant blooms only once, then dies. It was doubtful if Grandfather Sakamaki would have buried anything so valuable near something that was not permanent.

"You probably have it all figured out," Ned remarked. "What's the answer?"

Nancy smiled. "I'm guessing that the identical symbols mean brothers and maybe even twins."

"Okay. Where does that get you?" Ned asked.

Nancy had to admit that at this point her theorizing had reached a dead end. "Maui is not a large place," she mused, "but on the other hand the island is not small, either. It's going to be a real challenge to find the two men if that's what the paper indicated."

Forty minutes later the pilot set his plane down at the Hana airport. A smiling Polynesian met them and introduced himself as Moki Kuano.

"Do you wish to stop at your hotel first or shall we go directly to the crater?" he asked.

"We don't want to miss anything," Bess spoke up. "What do you advise?"

The Hawaiian guide smiled. "Perhaps we should go to the crater first. It is a long drive, but we should get there by sunset, and if we are lucky, you may see the Specter of Brocken."

"What's that?" Burt inquired.

The guide explained that it was a phenomenon viewed from the rim of the crater when it was filled with clouds. "You'll see your reflection in a rainbow which circles the clouds."

"Sounds spooky and wonderful!" Bess remarked.

Moki suggested that the travelers check their bags at the airport. He would come back for them later. The group agreed, since with eight in the car there was no room for luggage.

"I understand that the crater is ten thousand feet above sea level," said Ned. "Will this car be able to take all of us up to it?"

There was a chuckle from Moki. "You just squeeze in. The car will do the rest."

The travelers managed to settle themselves comfortably though crowded in the tourist car. All of them were charmed with the old tree-shaded city of Hana, a cultural center of ancient

Hawaii. Nancy learned that several retired professors and other students of volcanology and Polynesian lore lived there. Instantly she thought of the symbols beneath the picture of the silversword plant.

"Maybe two men live here who can help me with the mystery!" she told herself excitedly.

Nancy's attention was diverted by Moki pointing out a gorgeous waterfall and she suddenly realized how long she had been daydreaming. They were far out of town!

On the way up the mountain, they passed fields of sugar cane and some of pineapple, but in the main this was ranch country with cattle grazing on lush grass. About two-thirds of the way to the top, Moki suddenly stopped the car.

"I will show you a silversword plant," he said.

Everyone alighted and followed him down a little incline over a gravelly, rocky section. Before them was the most amazing plant the visitors had ever seen. It stood some ten feet in the air. From the lower part of the stalk grew a shower of leaves which looked like hairy silver swords. Moki explained that hairs on the leaves kept out the sun's rays and prevented moisture escaping from the plant.

The upper six feet of the plant was the flower itself. From the center stalk grew green foliage and hundreds of purple and yellow flowers.

"Exquisite!" Hannah Gruen exclaimed. "This

is certainly worth coming miles and miles to see."

Moki said that the mainlanders were fortunate. This was not a spot where the plants usually grew. Smiling, he added that he thought this one had deliberately planted itself away from the crater proper to show off its beauty to the passers-by on the road.

After the group had gazed at it in awe awhile, walking around the unusual plant several times, Moki said they must be on their way. The car climbed up the mountainside. When it finally reached the top, Nancy and her friends walked to the rim, and stood breathless at the magnificent spectacle before them. Holding onto an iron railing, they gazed down into an enormous depression. Part of it was grassy with plants growing on the lava floor. But most amazing were the series of cinder cones, some as high as eight hundred feet, which Moki said were the result of volcanic eruptions. The whole scene was bathed in the glow of a brilliant red sunset.

For a long time, the group stood speechless as Moki explained that the crater was seven miles long and two miles wide. So interested were the sight-seers that they hardly noticed the clouds gathering over the crater. In a short time the area was filled with them and suddenly a complete rainbow surrounded the clouds.

"And look!" Bess cried out, pointing. "There's my reflection in the center of them!"

"And you do look like a spook," George remarked.

Every one of the visitors was clearly reflected among the clouds.

Nancy and George were particularly intrigued. Trying to see more from another vantage point, they walked a distance out on the cliff beyond the railing.

George went a few steps ahead of Nancy. Gazing into the clouds and not watching where she was going, she suddenly lost her balance.

Nancy, seeing this, made a wild grab for her and caught hold of George's blouse. But the weight of George's body dragged the two of them over the side of the cliff!

CHAPTER XVII

Volcano Birds

THE INSTANT the two girls started tumbling down the cliffside, the three boys jumped to the rescue. They were beside Nancy and George in a moment, bracing themselves against the steep slope, and asking if the girls had been injured.

"Only my pride," George replied. "What a dumb thing to do!"

Since both she and Nancy felt shaken up and had suffered a few bruises, it was decided that the group would leave at once and go to the ranch motel outside of Hana where they had reservations. It was nearly dusk when they arrived at the attractive mountainside inn with its low, rustic buildings.

Bess was glad that dinner was ready. "I'm starving," she said, as they all sat down at a long table.

The table was very attractive with a centerpiece

of gardenias floating in a bowl of monkeypod wood. At each setting was a large slice of papaya, covered with chunks of pineapple, banana, and mango, and sprinkled with shredded coconut.

"I'm sure going to miss these tropical fruits when I get back to Emerson," Burt said with a laugh. "Fellows, can you imagine our dinners at college starting with a course like this?"

Ned and Dave grinned. "Bean soup is usually what they start with," Dave told the others.

There was a great deal of banter and teasing during the meal. But directly afterward, Nancy became serious. She told her friends that she had been doing some thinking about the drawing found in the chest. It had occurred to her that possibly there were two men—perhaps twins—in Hana, who were interested in some specific way in silversword plants.

Excusing herself, she left the others and asked the hotel clerk at the desk if he knew of anyone who was particularly interested in the plant. He replied that he did not, but that perhaps the manager, Mr. Blake, might know. He ushered Nancy into an inner office and introduced her to the manager.

Nancy again asked her question. Mr. Blake did not hesitate a moment. "Yes, there are two such men here in town. They're twins, and professors. The Anderson brothers have made a special study of the silversword plant."

A surge of excitement swept over Nancy. Her clue was about to bring results!

"The Anderson brothers retired from teaching some time ago," Mr. Blake went on. "Since studying our silversword plant and finding that it grows nowhere else in the world, they have come up with a very interesting theory."

Mr. Blake said the professors believed that the original seeds had been shot from space when the planet earth was being formed, and that they had lain dormant in this locale until the Hawaiian Island group was erupted.

Nancy was astounded at this theory, and eager to talk to the professors about it.

"Are the Andersons willing to have visitors?" she asked Mr. Blake.

"Oh, yes, indeed," the manager answered.

"If they have a phone," said Nancy, "perhaps I could call them and make an appointment."

The hotel manager reached for a copy of the telephone directory, found the number, and put in the call for Nancy. A deep voice at the other end of the wire said, "Nils Anderson speaking."

"This is Mr. Blake at the motel," the manager told him. "We have a guest here, Miss Nancy Drew, who would like to speak to you."

He handed the phone to Nancy, who said, "Hello. This is Nancy Drew from River Heights on the mainland." Then she asked, "Professor Anderson, did you know a man in Honolulu named Nikkio Sakamaki who lived at Kaluakua?"

"My brother and I knew him well," came the reply.

"Then may I please come to see you?" the young sleuth inquired. "My father is attorney for Mr. Sakamaki's grandson. A mystery has arisen in connection with his grandfather's estate and perhaps you can help in solving it."

Professor Anderson chuckled. "I love mysteries and I should be very happy to see you. Can you come here about nine-thirty tomorrow morning?"

Nancy said she could and later asked Ned to go with her. They arrived at the Anderson cottage promptly and were admitted by the brothers, who were identical twins. The white-haired men were about seventy years old, tall and straight, with ruddy complexions and twinkling blue eyes.

Nancy and Ned introduced themselves, and Ned revealed that Nancy was doing some detective work for her father in connection with the Sakamaki case."

"That's very interesting," one of the men said.

The professors then introduced themselves. Nils was a botanist, Stephen a zoologist. "We came from California originally," said Stephen, "but we lived in Honolulu for many years and lectured occasionally at the University."

His twin took up the story. "We became acquainted with Mr. Sakamaki of Kaluakua because of his interest in science. He was a very well-informed man, especially on the subject of botany. We three became great friends and saw a good deal of one another until Stephen and and I decided to come to Hana and make a study of the silversword plant."

"Mr. Blake told us about your theory as to the way the seeds got to this earth," Nancy spoke up.

Nils nodded. "It seems like the only logical explanation," he said, "but we have a great deal more studying to do and it is possible we'll change our minds."

Nancy now told the professors further details of her father's connection with the Sakamaki case, and also about her own interest in the puzzle.

"We've been trying hard to clear up the mystery," she said, "and just came upon a new clue." She explained about the discovery of the chest with the drawing of the silversword plant and the symbols meaning men. "Are you the men indicated?" she asked, smiling.

Neither of the twins replied at once. Instead, they gazed at each other for several moments as if trying to decide how to answer. But finally Nils spoke up.

"Old Nikkio Sakamaki was full of fun and incidentally full of sage Oriental sayings. He took great pleasure in thinking up clues to the solution of the Kaluakua mystery. He always said he wanted his heir to work to unfathom it."

As the elderly man stopped speaking, Nancy asked again, "And did one of the clues lead to you people because you can tell us something?"

Stephen smiled. "You have guessed correctly, Miss Drew. Mr. Sakamaki said if anyone should ever ask questions similar to the ones which you have put that we were to answer, 'Watch the angel birds over Mauna Loa.'"

"'Watch the angel birds over Mauna Loa,'" Nancy repeated. "Does that mean the volcano Mauna Loa?"

The professors grinned delightedly. Then Nils answered, "We were instructed to say no more."

It was clear to Nancy that they had no intention of breaking any promise they had given old Mr. Sakamaki. Tactfully she changed the subject and asked the Andersons if they knew whether Nikkio Sakamaki had ever mentioned having a wife and child in California.

"No, he never did," Nils replied. "In fact, I believe he was in California only a few days before coming to Honolulu."

Nancy was so excited to hear this that she almost jumped out of her chair. "This is very important news," she said. "A brother and sister from California have arrived in Honolulu to claim two-thirds of the estate. They say they are grandchildren of Grandfather Sakamaki."

Once more the brothers looked at each other for several moments before speaking. Then Nils said, "I am amazed to hear this and doubt the story very much. I believe I may be able to help you prove that these people are impostors."

"Oh, if you only could!" Nancy cried out.

Nils Anderson went on to say that old Mr. Sakamaki had given him several letters containing data about rare Japanese flowers. These letters had been written to Mr. Sakamaki while he was still in Japan.

"He had no further use for them," the professor explained, "and since he knew I would like to study the letters and could read Japanese, he gave them to me. If my memory serves me correctly, the dates on those letters might prove that Mr. Sakamaki was in Japan at the time these people claim he was married and living in California."

Nancy was almost beside herself with elation. "Do you have these letters here?" she said eagerly.

"Not in Hana," Nils Anderson replied. "When we moved here, I put them in the bank vault in Honolulu." Seeing the excitement on Nancy's face, he smiled and added, "I'll be very happy to fly to Honolulu and look at the letters. If I am right in my assumption, I'll turn the letters over to the executors of Mr. Sakamaki's estate."

"That's very kind, and certainly wonderful news," said Nancy.

Professor Anderson smiled. "Before getting in touch with the executor, I'll call you on the phone. Will you be at Kaluakua?"

For an instant Nancy toyed with the idea of returning immediately to Honolulu and awaiting his call. But she decided to postpone the trip back until she had gone to the island of Hawaii and watched the angel birds flying over Mauna Loa. She *must* figure out the next clue to the secret of Kaluakua! She told her plan to the professor, who said he would put off his flight to Honolulu a day.

The following morning Nancy decided to telephone Kiyabu and tell him of the trip to Hawaii and also find out what had been going on at the estate. The caretaker told her that no messages had come from anyone, including Mr. Drew.

"We are having bad luck here," Kiyabu reported. "Mr. Jerral was taken ill soon after dinner the day you left. He has been confined to his bed ever since. Mr. Chatley had a doctor for him."

"Then that means he has not been able to keep watch on Roy Chatley and his sister," Nancy remarked.

"I am afraid not," Kiyabu replied, "but I have been guarding the place the best I could. Emma has been helping me, too."

"Are your guests enjoying themselves?" Nancy asked.

An exclamation of disgust came from Kiyabu. "Miss Drew, those people are impossible. Always they are ordering me to go on errands. I am sure they want me to leave the estate for good. Then they have harsh words for Emma and me and they have threatened us several times."

"How dreadful!" Nancy exclaimed.

"But that part is not so bad as the rest," the caretaker went on. "Mrs. Lee and Mr. Chatley have had company here all the time. The people who come are very rough. They have broken much furniture. Emma and I have put away all the small pieces we could."

Nancy tried to express her sympathy and say that she and her friends would return immediately, but she had no chance. Kiyabu talked fast and loud in his excitement.

"The men make jokes all the time. They say they want double of eggs and double of coffee. One of them even ordered double cakes of soap for his bathroom. And every time one of them says this, the rest of them laugh so loud it hurts my ears."

The distraught caretaker went on with his tale of woe, saying how sick poor Mr. Jerral was and what were he and Emma going to do? But Nancy did not answer. A sudden thought had come to her which made her instinctively clutch at her throat.

Were Janet Lee and Roy Chatley knowingly entertaining members of the Double Scorps at Kaluakua?

CHAPTER XVIII

An Explosion

KIYABU continued to complain bitterly of the unseemly doings at Kaluakua. "Those visitors played some crazy game in the garden and ruined some of my rare plants!" he cried out in despair. "And Mr. Sakamaki was so proud of his flowers!"

Nancy was indignant. Her thoughts traveled to Mr. Jerral. Why had he permitted this? Was he too ill to object? Why had he not sent for a replacement?

It occurred to her that possibly Mr. Jerral was not so ill as he seemed to be—that he was using this method to allay any suspicion on the part of the "guests" at Kaluakua, and actually was watching them very intently. Nevertheless, she offered to return to the estate at once.

"That will not be necessary, Miss Nancy," Kiyabu said. "We will manage somehow."

"Do you think," Nancy questioned, "that Roy Chatley's guests are searching for something?"

"No, I do not," Kiyabu replied. "I just think they are here to have a good time. But they have very bad manners."

"In any case, we'll be home late tomorrow," Nancy promised. "If things get too bad, I suggest you call the police."

After the young sleuth hung up, she kept wondering whether or not she had made the right decision in not going directly home. When she discussed it with the others in her group, they urged Nancy to go to the island of Hawaii to see the angel birds. Moki and a friend of his drove them to the airport in two cars.

"I have a friend in Hawaii who is a fine guide as well as taxi driver," Moki told them. "When you arrive at the airport in Hilo, ask for Keaka."

"We'll do that," said Ned. "Thanks, Moki."

Upon their arrival at Hilo three-quarters of an hour later, Nancy and Ned questioned the taxi drivers until they found Keaka. He was a small, dark, pleasant man about forty years of age.

"Yes, I can take you for a trip at once and give you as much time as you like," he said. "I am grateful to my friend Moki for sending you to me."

Learning that they would be able to stay only until the following afternoon, he suggested a general sight-seeing tour at once. They could stay overnight at the Volcano House, and take a look at Mauna Loa the next morning.

Keaka's car was a station wagon, so there was plenty of room for everyone. Part of the luggage was strapped to the roof. Then everyone got in.

"Have you ever heard of our Fern Forest?" Keaka asked.

Ned said that he had read that the ferns were really as high as trees.

Keaka laughed. "You shall judge for yourself," he answered, and drove off.

The city of Hilo itself was a busy place, with a fine harbor where steamers unloaded all types of freight. One of the most interesting sections of the waterfront was the bulk-sugar storage plant.

Keaka suggested that they look around inside. He led the way into the building and up a twisting flight of iron steps. At the top was a catwalk from which one could look down into the huge sugar storage vats.

"This place can receive more than three hundred tons of sugar an hour and can load freighters at the rate of six hundred tons an hour," their guide told them.

"Astounding!" remarked Hannah Gruen.

Two of the bins were filled with brown raw sugar which Keaka said would be refined in California. The other bins were empty.

"You could practically set the Empire State Building from New York City in one of these," George remarked.

"You sure could," Burt agreed. Then, grinning, he said, "I'd say this is the sweetest place on earth."

The others smiled, and Bess commented, "Also one of the hottest. Let's go! I'd prefer the cool Fern Forest."

Keaka drove them through attractive residential sections, and finally out of town. Soon the car began to climb, and after a time reached a road running directly through a forest area made up almost exclusively of giant ferns.

"They really are as tall as trees!" Bess cried out excitedly. "Oh, let's get out and take some pictures."

"Watch out for snakes," Mrs. Gruen warned.

"That won't be necessary," the guide spoke up. "There are no poisonous land snakes on these islands."

Hannah sighed in relief and the sight-seers alighted. They walked a short distance into the forest. The giant ferns were surprisingly sturdy and George with a chuckle said, "Hypers, what a fan one of these would make!"

The group snapped some interesting pictures of the giant ferns, then Keaka suggested they go on. At times they passed through forests of trees and ferns and at other times through open country. Finally after a long, gradual climb the road brought them to a large green plateau.

"We are in the Kilauea Crater now," the guide announced.

Presently he stopped the car at the side of the road and suggested that the passengers follow him. He headed for a spot where they could see steam issuing from the ground.

"I'll show you some burning water," he said mysteriously.

"Burning water?" Bess repeated. Keaka smiled but did not explain further.

Soon the group reached a circular pit in the ground about six feet in diameter. Through the drifting steam, the tourists could see water several feet below.

"O-oh, this smells horrid," said Bess.

"Sure does," Dave agreed.

Keaka smiled but made no comment. From his pocket he took a book of matches and lighted one.

"Here goes!" he called, still grinning. "Look out, everybody!"

He threw the match down into the water. Instead of being extinguished, the flame instantly caused a small explosion. The group fell back in dismay as yellow-and-red flames shot up a distance of some six inches above the ground.

"Why, that's dangerous!" Hannah cried out.

Nancy laid an affectionate arm around the woman's shoulders. "I'm sure Keaka wouldn't do it if it were dangerous." Turning to the guide, she saw that he was lighting another match. He threw this too down toward the water. Once more there was an explosion and flames shot up!

"What causes such a reaction?" Ned asked him.

Keaka explained that hydrogen sulfide gas was being formed continuously below the earth's surface and found its escape with the steam. It ignited when fire came in contact with the fumes.

"Is gas part of what starts an eruption?" Ned inquired.

"Yes. Gases are contained in the seething, boiling molten rock underground. After a while, if they cannot find any release, pressure is built up. When this becomes too great, an eruption occurs —which happens now and then over on Mauna Loa. But around here there are so many vents in the ground that the gas has no trouble getting out."

Bess looked a little puzzled. "You mean that the pressure of the gases forces the molten rock to burst out of the earth and that's how volcanoes erupt?"

"Exactly," the guide replied. "If you're lucky, you may see an eruption on Mauna Loa while you're here."

"Oh, I hope not," said Bess fearfully. "We might be buried under that scorching lava!"

Keaka laughed and shook his head. "We have some of the world's finest geologists here," he said. "They have many ways of telling when there will be an eruption and nobody gets too close."

Despite his reassuring words, Bess continued to worry that a volcano might expode right before

The flame instantly caused a small explosion

her eyes. It was not until they reached the delightful Volcano House, and she had eaten a delicious meal, that she forgot her fear.

After supper the visitors from the mainland walked around the attractively planted grounds, marveling at the steam coming out of the ground in many spots.

"This is the most exciting place I've ever visited," George remarked to Nancy. "I'm glad Bess is over her fright about volcanoes. I feel a little bit myself as if some trick might be played on the people around here by that goddess Pele."

Ned, overhearing the remark, said he had been talking with a volcanologist from the Hawaiian National Park Service. The man had stated there was absolutely no danger.

"By the way, he invited us to come over to headquarters tomorrow morning and see colored motion pictures of the most recent eruption at Mauna Loa."

"Let's go!" Nancy urged.

When Keaka appeared with the station wagon the next morning, Nancy told him of the invitation. The guide said by all means they must view the movie and drove them to the headquarters building.

For half an hour they were captivated by one of the most fantastic motion pictures they had ever seen. Fountains of red-and-yellow lava were shot high into the air, then came down to run as a burning river all the way to the sea. Upon reaching water, lava and ocean met in a hissing roar, sending up volumes of steam ten thousand feet into the air.

"No lives were lost during this eruption," the narrator explained, "but a couple of dozen buildings were, and more than a mile of highway was buried. It is estimated that a billion tons of lava flowed from beneath the surface of the earth."

Nancy and her friends left the headquarters building awestruck by the thought of what Mother Nature can do. Keaka drove them to the scene depicted in the movie. How different it seemed now! The site was gray and harmless looking. As they drove along, the guide pointed out where the streams of lava had run down to the sea. Directing their attention to the various scooped-out, cone-shaped hills, he said:

"Those bowllike depressions are called *caldera*."

Finally they came to the main crater of Mauna Loa. Standing on the edge, the group looked down into a blackish-gray depth, seamed with fissures, some narrow, some wide.

"And there are the angel birds!" Nancy cried out.

Swooping low one moment and disappearing the next were the little white birds. Nancy gazed at them intently. What was their secret which Grandfather Sakamaki was trying to indicate to his grandson to help him solve the mystery of Kaluakua?

"Those birds," Keaka spoke up, "are man's friends. It seems as if they have been put here for a real purpose. It's said they can detect when there is going to be an eruption and fly far away."

Nancy studied their motions for a long time. She was particularly fascinated by the way they fluttered, almost like butterflies, over one area, then swooped or rose, and fluttered again over another area.

Suddenly the young sleuth snapped her fingers. "I think I know what Grandfather Sakamaki meant!" she declared.

CHAPTER XIX

A King's Treasure

"You've guessed the mystery?" Bess asked, astounded.

"Oh, no," Nancy answered, "but I think I know what the clue of the angel birds means. I believe that Nikkio Sakamaki was telling his grandson to fly over the estate."

As Keaka strolled off toward the station wagon, Nancy quickly explained to her friends, "If we swoop down low over the Golden Pavilion, I'm sure that we will find either another clue or perhaps the answer to the riddle."

"It sounds reasonable," Bess remarked. "But what are you going to swoop down in?"

George answered. "A plane, of course, silly."

Nancy was thoughtful for several moments, then suggested a plan. "I think I should return in secret to Kaluakua, perhaps with Ned, and see what we can find out. Suppose one of you phone there and say that the group has postponed their return until tomorrow morning. The Chatleys and their friends will assume that this includes Ned and me. In the meantime, we'll do some quiet sleuthing."

Ned was enthusiastic about the idea. He was eager to start at once, but Nancy reminded him that it would be far better to cruise slowly over the Golden Pavilion in a helicopter than to fly over it in a plane. They would have to make arrangements to charter one.

"Do you think Keaka could be trusted to help us?" Ned asked Nancy. "He probably knows some helicopter pilots."

Nancy thought this was a good suggestion. But before taking up the matter with Keaka she went on to tell the others more of her plan. "After we get to Honolulu, Ned and I will stay with the Armstrongs. If anything comes up, phone me there. And I'll call you at the Volcano House."

Hannah was concerned about Nancy's undertaking this bit of detective work, and made Nancy and Ned promise that they would be extremely careful. At that moment Keaka walked back to the group and Nancy asked about helicopter service to Oahu.

The Hawaiian smiled. "I know just the man to take you," he said. "We'll drive back to Park Headquarters and I will phone him for you."

When they reached the building, Keaka went inside and was gone so long that Nancy began to feel discouraged about the project. But presently the guide appeared, a broad grin on his face.

"Everything is arranged," he announced. "Ken Brown will be waiting with his helicopter at four o'clock at the Hilo airport."

"Thank you very much," said Nancy, then suggested that they all return to the Volcano House for luncheon and to make arrangements for the others to spend the night there.

At three o'clock Nancy and Ned drove off with Keaka. When they reached the Hilo airport, he introduced them to Ken Brown. The pilot was a tall, slender mainlander with a blond crew cut and flashing blue eyes.

"A secret mission, eh?" he asked, grinning. "Sounds good. Climb in."

Nancy and Ned shook hands with Keaka, thanked him again for all his help, and wished him well. Then they climbed aboard. The great rotors began to whirl and in a short time the helicopter was air-borne. As they neared the tip of Oahu, Ned told the pilot exactly where Kaluakua was located.

"Suppose we go past it first and then decide from which angle to approach the pavilion," Ken suggested.

"Good idea," Ned replied. "We can see if anyone is out in the gardens."

"Yes," Nancy agreed. "We'd prefer that nobody realize we're purposely flying over the estate."

Ken kept to the shore line. As they came opposite the Golden Pavilion, Nancy cried out, "Ned, look! I never noticed that the flower bed down there is in the shape of a plumiera blossom! Also, one petal is a little longer than the others. It points directly to the secret doorway under the pavilion."

No one was visible on the grounds and in a moment Nancy asked the pilot to turn around and this time fly as low as possible over the Golden Pavilion. He did so, and as he came back, Nancy and Ned watched intently. From the air, the golden roof, in the form of a plumiera flower, shone brilliantly in the sunlight.

"I didn't see anything unusual, did you?" Ned asked, as Ken sped on.

"No, I didn't," Nancy replied. "Ken, could you fly a little lower and a little slower?"

The young pilot grinned. "Anything to please," he called back.

This time when Ken went over the Golden Pavilion it seemed as if he was only a few feet from it, and went so slowly that Nancy and Ned were able to give the flower roof a close scrutiny.

"Ned!" Nancy cried excitedly. "I see it!"

"See what?" he asked, puzzled.

"That symbol right in the center of the flower!" Nancy explained excitedly. "Oh, Ken, please fly over it once more."

As the helicopter made a wide sweep and came back over the roof of the Golden Pavilion, Nancy and Ned gazed intently at the symbol which Nancy had spotted. Quickly she sketched the symbol in her note pad, then began riffling the pages of the book.

"Have you seen enough?" Ken called back. "I just saw somebody come out of the house. The folks in there may become suspicious."

"I've seen enough," Nancy replied. "Please take us to the airport." She continued to look through the notebook until she came to a certain page. On it were a number of Polynesian symbols and their translations. "I've been collecting these," she told Ned.

"From books?" he inquired.

Nancy said that she had copied them from various places—objects in the museum, pieces of furniture, and advertisements. "Oh, Ned!" she suddenly exclaimed excitedly. "Here it is!"

She pointed to one of the symbols, comparing it with the drawing she had just made. "It matches! And it means king!"

"Good sleuthing," Ned commented. "But where do we go from here?"

"I believe," said Nancy, her eyes sparkling,

"that some treasure belonging to an ancient Hawaiian king is hidden at the center of the golden plumiera."

"If you're right," said Ned, "you're about to solve one of the most intriguing mysteries in your career."

Nancy admitted that she could hardly wait to investigate the roof of the pavilion. By the time they had landed and taken a taxi to the Armstrongs' home, she had formulated a plan of action. "Tonight you and I will go secretly to the Golden Pavilion with a ladder, Ned. You're to have the honor of uncovering the treasure. I'll protect you by being a dancing ghost in the moonlight."

Ned's brow wrinkled. "I don't get it."

Nancy said that what she hoped to do was scare away anyone in the house or on the grounds who might see the "ghost," and so leave Ned free to carry on his work.

"The person may not run away, of course, but I hope at least he won't come near."

Ned laughed softly. "Light begins to dawn. You're going to pretend to be that ghostlike hula dancer? The one who was supposed to frighten people away?"

"Exactly, Ned. Of course, I may run into trouble if she, too, happens to come around, or if she's staying at Kaluakua. But we'll have to take that chance. Whatever happens, I'll try to give you plenty of time to find the treasure."

Ned remarked that it would not be safe to leave the ladder against the building, once he was on the roof. Anyone approaching the pavilion would know at once that someone was up there.

"I'll hide the ladder while you're working," Nancy promised.

Ned grinned. "You'd better not let anything go wrong and leave me stranded up on that roof!" he warned.

By this time the taxi had reached the Armstrongs' home. Mrs. Armstrong opened the door.

"Oh, I'm so glad to see you!" she cried out. "Hannah Gruen telephoned that you were coming. When I heard something of your plan, I began to worry, but now that you're here safe, I guess everything is all right."

She showed Nancy and Ned to rooms which they would occupy for the night, then suggested that they all meet in the garden for cool drinks of lemonade.

"Would you mind," Nancy asked, "if we stay indoors? I don't want anyone to know we're here."

"Why certainly, dear," Mrs. Armstrong said. "We'll talk in the living room."

Mr. Armstrong had been out, but had returned by the time Nancy and Ned had freshened up. The older couple listened intently as Nancy unfolded her plan.

"And now," she asked at the conclusion, "do you

know where I can find a lightweight folding ladder that could be put inside your car, Mr. Armstrong?"

The man thought for a moment, then said he remembered their carpenter had one. He would phone and find out if they might borrow it. While he was gone, Nancy inquired if Mrs. Armstrong had a white muumuu and some white veils which she might borrow.

"Come upstairs with me," her hostess said. "I think we can locate something."

Mrs. Armstrong rummaged through a bureau drawer, pulling out everything that was white. Among the articles were two white scarfs.

"And here is a white muumuu!" she said delightedly. "We'll press these things in a jiffy and you'll be all set for your part as a hula ghost dancer."

When she and Nancy returned to the first floor, Mr. Armstrong said, "I have permission for you to borrow the ladder. I'll run over and get it now."

"That's wonderful!" said Nancy, "and I have my costume."

She insisted upon pressing the muumuu and scarfs herself while Mrs. Armstrong sat by in the laundry room and chatted with her. Ned, meanwhile, had found a record player and was enjoying a variety of Hawaiian tunes.

Dinner was served indoors, so that no prying

eyes would see Nancy and Ned. Conversation was both jolly and serious. As the time neared for Nancy and Ned to leave, the youth filled his two jacket pockets with several small tools to help pry up the center of the golden flower roof. Mr. Armstrong brought the car to the door, and the couple slipped into it.

"Good luck!" said Mr. and Mrs. Armstrong in a low tone.

On the way to Kaluakua, Nancy and Ned discussed the possibility of entering the grounds secretly.

"That's easy," said Ned. "I'll park down beyond the gardens in a grove of trees I've seen. There's a hidden path through it to the beach. We can come up alongside the bushes from the beach, and then turn in toward the pavilion."

"Good!" Nancy approved. After Ned had parked the car, she said, "I'll follow you."

Ned carried the ladder. Over Nancy's arm hung the muumuu and scarfs. Ned's directions proved to be correct, and after a considerable walk, they arrived in a woodsy garden near the Golden Pavilion.

The ladder was set against the side of the building which was in shadow, and Ned scrambled nimbly up. When he reached the roof, he lay flat and crawled to the center.

In the meantime, Nancy had folded the ladder and dragged it to a place of hiding among the bushes. She looked around and listened. There was no sound, but far down the beach she could see a moving light.

"I'd better get into this costume," she told herself. "Someone may be coming here."

Hurriedly she slipped the muumuu over her head, removed her shoes and stockings, then draped the two scarfs gracefully around her head and shoulders in such a way that she could cover her face if necessary. Stepping out from the shadows, she noticed that the moving light was a little closer.

Her heart pounding, she began to hum a Hawaiian melody and dance the hula. As she swayed and raised her arms from side to side, the young sleuth kept wondering how Ned was making out. In playing her part of the ghost dancer, she dared not look up nor wander far away from the pavilion.

Suddenly the moving light on the beach went out. Had the person carrying it spotted her? Had he been frightened by the apparition, or was he stealthily moving toward her? For a moment Nancy felt like running, but her courage returned.

"I mustn't desert Ned," she commanded herself.

She continued to dance over the grass, up the steps of the pavilion, and across the floor. She glided down the steps on the other side. Still no one came to disturb her.

"Surely Ned will be ready in a minute," Nancy thought.

A second later she was startled by a voice which seemed to hiss at her from only a short distance away. At first she thought it was Ned, then she detected the figure of a man emerging from among the bushes. Nancy's heart missed a beat but she continued her acting, holding one of the scarfs across her face.

"Keep on dancing while I talk," the stranger ordered, "and for ten minutes after I leave. Kiyabu is afraid of you and he won't come while you're here."

Nancy was elated. Her ruse was working!

The man sat down on the ground and began strumming his fingers on the edge of the pavilion steps. Suddenly he raised his two forefingers and touched them together.

Nancy almost cried aloud. But she kept on dancing as she said to herself, "This man must be Jim O'Keefe!"

In a few moments he began to speak again. "It's a good thing you showed up tonight, Milly," the man said. "If you'd decided to welsh on us, your life and that of your double-crossin' husband wouldn't have lasted long."

Nancy pretended to shiver and the man gave a low, sardonic laugh. "Now listen. Tomorrow night you're to repeat this dance. Nancy Drew and the rest of her gang put off returnin' until tomorrow. They'll come out to watch you and then we'll nab 'em all."

O'Keefe went on to say that Nancy's group would be taken to a mountain cabin, tied up, and left to starve. "Sakamaki will come next," the man said harshly. "In the meantime, we'll all clear out but the grandchildren." He guffawed sardonically. "We'll leave them to get control of the estate for us!"

Nancy, as Milly, made no reply. She continued to dance. O'Keefe got up, laughed softly, and went off toward the house.

"I guess we got here just in time," Nancy told herself.

When the ten minutes were up, Ned came to the edge of the roof.

"I heard everything. Let's get out of here as fast as possible!" Then he added jubilantly, "I have the king's treasure!"

Nancy rushed off to get the ladder, set it in place, and Ned hurried down the rungs. Over his arm he was carrying a long, varicolored cape made of birds' feathers.

"Why, this is one of those ceremonial capes made from the extinct o-o bird!" Nancy exclaimed softly. "A museum piece!"

"It sure was well protected," Ned commented. "I had to pry up a lot of insulation. That's what took me so long!" He threw the cape over his shoulders and strutted around.

"It's simply gorgeous!" Nancy whispered.

At this instant the couple heard footsteps. Nancy and Ned began to run. Nancy had no time to put on her shoes and stockings, and Ned found it impossible to carry the ladder. He dropped it among some bushes and the two sped off.

But they were too late. The next instant they were surrounded by four men.

Ned managed to knock out one of the men, but the odds were against the couple.

The ancient cape was taken away from Ned, and he and Nancy were bound and gagged. Two of the captors dragged their prisoners back to the Golden Pavilion, opened the secret panel in the foundation, and roughly pushed them inside. The door was slammed shut!

CHAPTER XX

Aloha!

UNABLE to speak and hardly able to move, Nancy and Ned could not express their anger aloud. But both were extremely annoyed at themselves for having been captured.

"We uncovered the secret only to have it snatched out of our hands at the last moment!" Nancy wailed silently.

Ned berated himself for not having protected Nancy better.

Both prisoners wriggled and rolled on the ground under the pavilion floor until they managed to remove their gags.

"Ned, where are you?" Nancy asked. "If you can answer, say something."

A second later the youth replied, "I'm over here." Apparently he was on the opposite side of their prison beneath the pavilion. "I think I can get these ropes off in a minute," Ned added.

But Nancy did not wait for him to accomplish it alone. She rolled over and over in the direction from which the sound of his voice had come. Reaching his side, she helped him untie the knots in the rope which pinioned his wrists behind his back. He, in turn, unfastened hers, then the two worked in pitch blackness to loosen the ropes which bound their ankles.

"This is a fine mess to be in!" said Ned. "Oh, Nancy, I should never have let you get in the clutches of these awful people."

Nancy begged him to stop worrying and suggested that they both try to find the secret opening. They went in opposite directions, feeling along the three-foot wall, until they met again halfway around.

"I didn't find anything," Ned reported. "How about you?"

"No luck," Nancy answered. "This time I guess we'd better make a slower circuit and go over every inch with our hands."

The two started off once more. They were almost at the halfway mark again when Nancy felt what seemed like a tiny crack. Hopefully she began following it with her finger tips.

"Ned," she said excitedly, "I think I've found the opening!"

He hurried toward her, and upon running his fingers over the crack, decided that this indeed was the secret door. Together he and Nancy pulled, pushed, and hammered on it. But the door did not budge.

"I'll try throwing my weight against it," Ned said.

Nancy crouched nearby, waiting hopefully. Ned, down on one knee like a football lineman about to charge his opponents, lunged. His shoulder thudded against the masonry.

"Oh, Ned," Nancy whispered, "you'll break a bone!"

Ned grimaced and tried it again. *Thump!* This time a tiny line of moonlight shone through.

"You've done it!" Nancy exclaimed with relief.

Ned made several more assaults on the stubborn piece of masonry, and finally the secret door gave way and swung outward.

"We'd better get away from here as fast as possible," Ned whispered.

"Oh, no!" Nancy objected. "Since our captors didn't return, they must think we're still neatly tied up. This is our chance to do a little sleuthing. I believe we may even be able to find out where the cape is and perhaps learn some other secrets. In fact, O'Keefe may be in the house."

Reluctantly, Ned agreed to do some more detective work with Nancy. First of all, she hunted for her shoes and stockings. Finding them, she put them on quickly, then the couple started off.

Keeping in the shadows as much as possible,

they crept toward the house. Several rooms were lighted.

"You keep guard," Nancy suggested to Ned. "I'll tiptoe up the back porch and look into the kitchen."

He nodded and she ascended the steps. As she peered inside the kitchen, Nancy gave a gasp of horror. Kiyabu and Emma, gagged and bound, were tied to chairs!

Nancy came quickly down the steps and whispered to Ned what she had seen. "Let's look in some of the other windows," she urged.

In the living room they saw signs of great activity. Seated in chairs were O'Keefe, the Ponds, Janet Lee, Roy Chatley, a reddish-blond man Nancy was sure must be Ralph Emler, a strange man, and three other women, one with a bandage on her arm.

"Well, Milly," Janet was saying to the woman with the bandage, "somebody ought to pin a medal on you."

"How about me?" the strange man spoke up. "I came along with her, didn't I? She's my wife. I deserve as much credit as she does."

More talk revealed to Nancy and Ned that Milly, the dancer, had been late in her appointment that evening. Instead of going to the Golden Pavilion to perform, she and her husband had driven directly to the house. That was how Nancy's subterfuge had been discovered! It was then that Milly told the others about the secret door that she had found.

"Oh, cut out this talk about medals," O'Keefe ordered. "We got to lay our plans for tomorrow morning."

In the meantime, Milly's husband had arisen and put on the feather cape. He began to parade around the room, speaking in nonsensical gibberish, as if imitating an ancient Hawaiian king.

"Take that off!" Roy Chatley ordered. "If anybody's going to wear it, O'Brien's the one. He's the king of us Double Scorps."

The man known as O'Keefe and O'Malley now got up from his chair and took the cape. "Yes," he said haughtily, "Mike O'Brien is head of this outfit and don't anybody forget it!"

Nancy's pulse was racing. Many questions relating to the mystery were being answered. But one angle of it still puzzled her. How did Roy Chatley and his sister fit into the picture? If they were going to inherit two-thirds of the estate, why were the Double Scorps going to get part of it?

"The only answer," the young sleuth told herself, "is that Janet and Roy really are impostors. Maybe Dad and Professor Nils Anderson will prove this. But we can't wait for them to get here. We must have this gang apprehended!"

Nancy wondered where Mr. Jerral was. As if

in answer to her thought, Mike O'Brien asked a man who had just entered the room:

"Well, Dr. Scribner, how's your patient?"

The physician laughed scornfully. "Oh, I just gave him another dose of medicine. It'll keep him on the sick list a while, then I'll give him some more!"

Nancy and Ned looked at each other in concern. So John Jerral had been deliberately made ill by the Double Scorps! The couple doubted that the man they called Dr. Scribner was a licensed physician at all. He, too, must be one of the gang!

Silently Nancy and Ned moved away from the window, drawing off to a little distance. They began to whisper and make plans for the capture of the Double Scorps.

"Let's go to Kiyabu's cottage and phone for the police," Nancy urged.

When Ned called headquarters, the astounded officer on duty said he would send a squad of men out at once. While waiting for them, Nancy called the Armstrongs and quickly related the night's adventure.

They in turn had some news for Nancy which delighted her. Mr. Drew, Mr. Sakamaki, and Professor Nils Anderson had just arrived at the Armstrong house. They would all drive out immediately.

Nancy relayed the information to Ned. "Soon

we'll know all the answers regarding the mystery of Kaluakua," she added.

Suddenly a worried expression crossed Ned's face. He quickly put a hand into his shirt pocket. As he pulled out a piece of paper, he looked relieved.

"I was afraid I had lost this," Ned explained. "I found it with the feather cape. I couldn't read very well in the moonlight, but I think it's important and must have something to do with the secret."

He opened it and together he and Nancy read the contents. It had been written by Grandfather Sakamaki and explained that the garment was a duplicate of a king's feather cape which had been given to one of his wife's ancestors as a special mark of favor. Since a king's cape was always buried with him, this duplicate was very valuable and had been hidden by the family, so that neither thieves nor conquerors from foreign lands would take it.

"My wife made me promise," Nikkio Sakamaki had written, "that I would never part with the cape. It became increasingly difficult to find a hiding place for it. Finally I thought of the idea of putting it under the center of the golden plumiera which would form the roof of a pavilion I was building."

The letter went on to say that he had decided

to make it difficult for his grandson to find the precious article, so he would always remember his Polynesian background, and the legends and symbols of ancient Hawaii. First, he had given the symbols of water and death to indicate that the Golden Pavilion near the water was the place to find the treasure. The symbol of death had indicated that the cape belonged to someone who had died.

The flower bed in the shape of a plumiera blossom, with one extra-long petal pointing to the secret door under the pavilion, was another clue. If his grandson managed to locate it, he would find the next clue, which in turn would lead him to the Anderson brothers, who knew the secret, then to the angel birds.

"But you, Nancy," said Ned proudly, "solved the mystery, not Nikkio Sakamaki's grandson."

Nancy laughed softly, then exclaimed, "Listen!"

There were sounds of footsteps outside. For a few brief moments, the couple feared that some of the Double Scorps were coming. But a moment later Nancy was in her father's arms, and Ned was shaking hands with Professor Nils Anderson, as Mr. and Mrs. Armstrong looked on, smiling broadly.

"The police are already here," Mr. Drew announced. "They were surrounding the house as we arrived, and I dare say that by this time they have captured the whole gang. Let's go and hear the confessions."

On the way to the big house, the lawyer gave a quick explanation of his work in Los Angeles.

"There were two Nikkio Sakamakis," he said. "Both came from Japan. The one with the San Francisco wife and daughter, who in turn had two children, Janet and Roy, was not our Mr. Sakamaki. These children, I learned, are not living, although this is not recorded in San Francisco. However, the couple who call themselves Janet and Roy had found out about this family and procured credentials to pose as grandchildren of Mr. Sakamaki of Kaluakua. They are not brother and sister, by the way, but husband and wife."

"Pretty slick team," Ned remarked.

"It was a plot of the whole Double Scorp gang," the lawyer said, and added that he might have had a difficult time proving his case, if it had not been for Professor Nils Anderson. The letters which he had taken from his safe-deposit box in Honolulu proved that Mr. Sakamaki of Kaluakua lived in Japan and was a single man at the time the impostors claimed he was in San Francisco and married.

When the group entered the house, members of the Double Scorps, surrounded by police, were all protesting their innocence. The captives stared in stupefaction and disbelief at Nancy and Ned.

"Yes, we escaped," said Nancy icily.

The sight of the couple and the fact that he had been outwitted by a girl unnerved Mike O'Brien completely. He readily confessed to his part in the scheme to get part or all of old Mr. Sakamaki's fortune.

He had shadowed the younger Mr. Sakamaki. Upon learning that he had engaged Mr. Drew, O'Brien had followed the lawyer and overheard the long luncheon conversation at which matters concerning the estate had been discussed.

"When I heard that all but the third-floor windows of the Drew home had burglar alarms, I decided to get hold of a ladder I could carry easy and one nobody would notice. By accident I saw a window washer using just the kind I wanted, so I rented it."

The king of the Double Scorps confessed taking the unusual jade ring from Homer Milbank. While he would not divulge the name and address of a friend who bought rare or old jewelry, he admitted that it was through him that he disposed of stolen pieces. There was time to take only the jade ring. He was astounded to learn, however, that the symbols on it were Polynesian.

"I'll bet that jewelry-buyer pal of yours is the one who came here the other day trying to get things cheap," Ned spoke up. "And Emler sold him the statuettes he stole from Grandpa Saka-maki."

O'Brien gave such a start that the others were sure Ned had hit upon the truth. He did not admit this, however. Instead he went on to say that after he learned Nancy had entered the case and was going to Honolulu, he had done everything to keep her from making the trip. He had stolen Togo, but the little dog had managed to get away.

"I had you followed from the Los Angeles airport," the Scorp said, "but the dumb guy I hired told me you shook him. And you did the same thing coming from the Honolulu airport."

Nancy asked O'Brien why he had bothered to follow the girls, but he would not answer. The young sleuth guessed that he probably intended to cause an accident to injure them and in this way keep her from reaching Kaluakua.

Another point which came up when the police gave Nancy, Ned, and their companions a chance to question the prisoners was that Emler often whistled to attract Kiyabu and Emma to the beach. While they were away from either the house or cottage, another member of the Double Scorps would start a search.

The gang had learned that there was some secret in connection with the estate and assumed it to be a treasure. Although they doubted that it would be at Kiyabu's cottage, they had thought they might find a letter or a clue of some kind to guide them to it.

"Did you find the secret entrance under the pavilion?" Nancy asked Milly, the dancer.

"Yes, I did," she answered. "Quite by chance, but I wasn't going to tell the others about it. I crawled under there hunting for the treasure. I didn't find anything, so I gave up searching." She gave the king of the Double Scorps a scorching look. "You've sure been mean to me, holding out on my share of money that was due me. If I'd found any fortune, I was going to run off with it."

"Okay, okay," interrupted one of the policemen. "Any more questions for the prisoners?" he asked.

Nancy said that she had some. "Who sent me the black lei with the poisoned tacks in it?"

O'Brien confessed that this had been his idea, although he had given the job to Ralph Emler. It was O'Brien himself who had thrown the fire tongs, in a desperate maneuver to keep Nancy from interfering further in the case.

All this time Kiyabu and Emma, who had been released, had been standing in a doorway, staring in amazement at the prisoners and listening to the story. Now the caretaker came forward to identify Milly's husband as the man who had come to him before Nancy's arrival to buy some of the valuable pieces at Kaluakua.

"But, Mr. Policeman," said Kiyabu, "I would not even show them. I had no right to sell them." He looked disgustedly at the Scorp. "When I wouldn't, he tried to bribe me."

Ned whispered to Nancy, "It's not hard to believe that."

She nodded as Kiyabu went on angrily, "I want to know why you broke down flowers and bushes and ruined part of the lawn."

O'Brien answered for the group. "We thought this might be a way of getting rid of you. Your boss would think you were a pretty poor caretaker and discharge you."

Mr. Sakamaki from River Heights gave the leader of the Double Scorps a withering look. "O'Brien, you guessed wrong on every count. And that includes Kiyabu and Emma. They are the most loyal and faithful people who could ever work for anyone. You might have learned many lessons of honesty and good manners from them."

The officer in charge of the police squad said that if there were no further questions the prisoners would be taken to jail. At that moment another officer came down the front stairs. He was introduced as a police surgeon.

"Mr. Jerral will suffer no permanent ill health from the drugs he was given by the gang," the surgeon reported. "He'll be up and around in a couple of days."

"Thank goodness for that," Nancy said quietly.

By this time the police had hustled the Double Scorps out of the house and herded them into several cars. Nancy and the others walked out to the porch to watch them drive off. As they were about to return inside, they heard voices coming from one side of the house. A moment later Bess, George, Burt, Dave, and Hannah Gruen hurried up the steps.

"We heard everything!" Bess exclaimed, hugging Nancy. "Oh, you wonderful, wonderful creature to solve this mystery!"

"That goes for all of you," Nancy declared.

George, paying no attention, cried out, "Three cheers for Nancy Drew!"

The young people gave three rousing cheers, then Nancy proposed three for Ned. "Wait until you hear all he did!" she said generously.

Hannah was a little more sedate in her kiss and hug for Nancy, but it was just as sincere. "Now at last I can stop worrying," she said. "That is, until the next mystery comes along."

Nancy herself knew this to be true. She would have adventures and Hannah would worry. Sooner than either of them expected, the young sleuth would be matching wits with the wiliest adversaries of her experience in *The Clue in the Old Stagecoach.*

The newcomers shook hands with Mr. Drew and were introduced to Professor Nils Anderson and Mr. Sakamaki. Bess then explained why they had come back early from Hawaii. "I had a hunch there would be excitement at Kaluakua and that we should return to take part in it."

She explained that they had caught a late plane and then called the Armstrongs. Getting no answer there, they had come directly to the estate. When they found the police in charge, they had decided to listen to the proceedings rather than interrupt.

Kiyabu had thrown the feather cape around Mr. Sakamaki who was loud in his praise of the Drews and their friends for recovering it and trapping the Double Scorps. "You went way beyond the line of duty—even risked your lives—to solve the secret of the Golden Pavilion.

"And my thanks to all of you also"—he beamed at the group—"that Kaluakua can be given to Honolulu as an outdoor theater. Tomorrow we shall celebrate with a great luau," the Hawaiian went on. "Perhaps we should arrange for some entertainment."

At once George spoke up. "Let's have our own entertainment," she suggested. "Ane Drew will dance the hula for us and Eluwene Nickerson will be crowned king and wear the feather cape!"

Nancy and Ned laughed and agreed.

Order Form
New revised editions of
THE BOBBSEY TWINS®

In *hardcover* at your local bookseller OR
simply mail in this handy order coupon and start your collection today!

Please send me the following Bobbsey Twins titles I've checked below.

AVOID DELAYS   Please Print Order Form Clearly

❏ 1	Of Lakeport	($5.99)	448-09071-6
❏ 2	Adventure in the Country	($5.95)	448-09072-4
❏ 6	On a Houseboat	($4.95)	448-09099-6
❏ 7	Mystery at Meadowbrook	($4.50)	448-09100-3
❏ 8	Big Adventure at Home	($4.50)	448-09134-8

Own the original exciting
BOBBSEY TWINS® ADVENTURE STORIES
still available:

❏13   Visit to the Great West   ($4.50)   448-08013-3

**VISIT PUTNAM BERKLEY ONLINE
ON THE INTERNET: http://www.putnam.com/berkley**

Payable in U.S. funds. No cash accepted. Postage & handling: $3.50 for one book. $1.00 for each additional. Maximum postage $8.50. Prices, postage and handling charges may change without notice. Visa, Amex, MasterCard call 1-800-788-6262, ext. 1, or fax 1-201-933-2316.

Or, check above books
and send this order form to:

**The Putnam Publishing Group
P.O. Box 12289, Dept. B
Newark, NJ 07101-5289**

Please allow 4-6 weeks for delivery.
Foreign and Canadian delivery 8-12 weeks

Bill my: ❏ Visa ❏ MasterCard ❏ Amex _____ (expires)

Card#_____

($10 minimum)

Daytime Phone # _____

Signature_____

Or enclosed is my: ❏ check ❏ money order
SHIP TO:

Book Total	$ _____
Applicable Sales Tax	$ _____
(CA, NJ, NY, GST Can.)	
Postage & Handling	$ _____
Total Amount Due	$ _____

Name _____

Address _____

City _____ State _____ Zip _____

BILL TO:
Name _____

Address _____

City _____ State _____ Zip _____

The Bobbsey Twins® Series is a trademark
of Simon & Schuster, Inc. and is registered
in the United States Patent and Trademark Office.

Order Form
Own the original 58 action-packed
HARDY BOYS MYSTERY STORIES®

In *hardcover* at your local bookseller OR
simply mail in this handy order coupon and start your collection today!

Please send me the following Hardy Boys titles I've checked below.
All Books Priced @ $5.99

AVOID DELAYS   Please Print Order Form Clearly

❑ 1	Tower Treasure	448-08901-7	❑ 30	Wailing Siren Mystery	448-08930-0
❑ 2	House on the Cliff	448-08902-5	❑ 31	Secret of Wildcat Swamp	448-08931-9
❑ 3	Secret of the Old Mill	448-08903-3	❑ 32	Crisscross Shadow	448-08932-7
❑ 4	Missing Chums	448-08904-1	❑ 33	The Yellow Feather Mystery	448-08933-5
❑ 5	Hunting for Hidden Gold	448-08905-X	❑ 34	The Hooded Hawk Mystery	448-08934-3
❑ 6	Shore Road Mystery	448-08906-8	❑ 35	The Clue in the Embers	448-08935-1
❑ 7	Secret of the Caves	448-08907-6	❑ 36	The Secret of Pirates Hill	448-08936-X
❑ 8	Mystery of Cabin Island	448-08908-4	❑ 37	Ghost at Skeleton Rock	448-08937-8
❑ 9	Great Airport Mystery	448-08909-2	❑ 38	Mystery at Devil's Paw	448-08938-6
❑ 10	What Happened at Midnight	448-08910-6	❑ 39	Mystery of the Chinese Junk	448-08939-4
❑ 11	While the Clock Ticked	448-08911-4	❑ 40	Mystery of the Desert Giant	448-08940-8
❑ 12	Footprints Under the Window	448-08912-2	❑ 41	Clue of the Screeching Owl	448-08941-6
❑ 13	Mark on the Door	448-08913-0	❑ 42	Viking Symbol Mystery	448-08942-4
❑ 14	Hidden Harbor Mystery	448-08914-9	❑ 43	Mystery of the Aztec Warrior	448-08943-2
❑ 15	Sinister Sign Post	448-08915-7	❑ 44	The Haunted Fort	448-08944-0
❑ 16	A Figure in Hiding	448-08916-5	❑ 45	Mystery of the Spiral Bridge	448-08945-9
❑ 17	Secret Warning	448-08917-3	❑ 46	Secret Agent on Flight 101	448-08946-7
❑ 18	Twisted Claw	448-08918-1	❑ 47	Mystery of the Whale Tattoo	448-08947-5
❑ 19	Disappearing Floor	448-08919-X	❑ 48	The Arctic Patrol Mystery	448-08948-3
❑ 20	Mystery of the Flying Express	448-08920-3	❑ 49	The Bombay Boomerang	448-08949-1
❑ 21	The Clue of the Broken Blade	448-08921-1	❑ 50	Danger on Vampire Trail	448-08950-5
❑ 22	The Flickering Torch Mystery	448-08922-X	❑ 51	The Masked Monkey	448-08951-3
❑ 23	Melted Coins	448-08923-8	❑ 52	The Shattered Helmet	448-08952-1
❑ 24	Short-Wave Mystery	448-08924-6	❑ 53	The Clue of the Hissing Serpent	448-08953-X
❑ 25	Secret Panel	448-08925-4	❑ 54	The Mysterious Caravan	448-08954-8
❑ 26	The Phantom Freighter	448-08926-2	❑ 55	The Witchmaster's Key	448-08955-6
❑ 27	Secret of Skull Mountain	448-08927-0	❑ 56	The Jungle Pyramid	448-08956-4
❑ 28	The Sign of the Crooked Arrow	448-08928-9	❑ 57	The Firebird Rocket	448-08957-2
❑ 29	The Secret of the Lost Tunnel	448-08929-7	❑ 58	The Sting of the Scorpion	448-08958-0

Also Available The Hardy Boys Detective Handbook 448-01990-6

VISIT PUTNAM BERKLEY ONLINE
ON THE INTERNET: http://www.putnam.com/berkley

Payable in U.S. funds. No cash accepted. Postage & handling: $3.50 for one book. $1.00 for each additional. Maximum postage $8.50. Prices, postage and handling charges may change without notice. Visa, Amex, MasterCard call 1-800-788-6262, ext. 1, or fax 1-201-933-2316.

Or, check above books
and send this order form to:

**The Putnam Publishing Group
P.O. Box 12289, Dept. B
Newark, NJ 07101-5289**

Bill my: ❑ Visa ❑ MasterCard ❑ Amex _____ (expires)

Card#_____
($10 minimum)

Daytime Phone # _____

Signature_____

Please allow 4-6 weeks for delivery.
Foreign and Canadian delivery 8-12 weeks

Or enclosed is my: ❑ check ❑ money order
SHIP TO:

Book Total $ _____
Name _____

Applicable Sales Tax $ _____
(CA, NJ, NY, GST Can.)
Address _____

Postage & Handling $ _____
City _____ State _____ Zip _____

Total Amount Due $ _____
BILL TO:
Name _____

Nancy Drew® and The Hardy Boys® are trademarks
of Simon & Schuster, Inc. and are registered
in the United States Patent and Trademark Office.
Address _____

City _____ State _____ Zip _____

Order Form
Own the original 56 thrilling
NANCY DREW MYSTERY STORIES®

In *hardcover* at your local bookseller OR
simply mail in this handy order coupon and start your collection today!

Please send me the following Nancy Drew titles I've checked below.
All Books Priced @ $5.99

AVOID DELAYS   Please Print Order Form Clearly

☐ 1 Secret of the Old Clock	448-09501-7	☐ 30 Clue of the Velvet Mask	448-09530-0
☐ 2 Hidden Staircase	448-09502-5	☐ 31 Ringmaster's Secret	448-09531-9
☐ 3 Bungalow Mystery	448-09503-3	☐ 32 Scarlet Slipper Mystery	448-09532-7
☐ 4 Mystery at Lilac Inn	448-09504-1	☐ 33 Witch Tree Symbol	448-09533-5
☐ 5 Secret of Shadow Ranch	448-09505-X	☐ 34 Hidden Window Mystery	448-09534-3
☐ 6 Secret of Red Gate Farm	448-09506-8	☐ 35 Haunted Showboat	448-09535-1
☐ 7 Clue in the Diary	448-09507-6	☐ 36 Secret of the Golden Pavilion	448-09536-X
☐ 8 Nancy's Mysterious Letter	448-09508-4	☐ 37 Clue in the Old Stagecoach	448-09537-8
☐ 9 The Sign of the Twisted Candles	448-09509-2	☐ 38 Mystery of the Fire Dragon	448-09538-6
☐ 10 Password to Larkspur Lane	448-09510-6	☐ 39 Clue of the Dancing Puppet	448-09539-4
☐ 11 Clue of the Broken Locket	448-09511-4	☐ 40 Moonstone Castle Mystery	448-09540-8
☐ 12 The Message in the Hollow Oak	448-09512-2	☐ 41 Clue of the Whistling Bagpipes	448-09541-6
☐ 13 Mystery of the Ivory Charm	448-09513-0	☐ 42 Phantom of Pine Hill	448-09542-4
☐ 14 The Whispering Statue	448-09514-9	☐ 43 Mystery of the 99 Steps	448-09543-2
☐ 15 Haunted Bridge	448-09515-7	☐ 44 Clue in the Crossword Cipher	448-09544-0
☐ 16 Clue of the Tapping Heels	448-09516-5	☐ 45 Spider Sapphire Mystery	448-09545-9
☐ 17 Mystery of the Brass-Bound Trunk	448-09517-3	☐ 46 The Invisible Intruder	448-09546-7
☐ 18 Mystery at Moss-Covered Mansion	448-09518-1	☐ 47 The Mysterious Mannequin	448-09547-5
☐ 19 Quest of the Missing Map	448-09519-X	☐ 48 The Crooked Banister	448-09548-3
☐ 20 Clue in the Jewel Box	448-09520-3	☐ 49 The Secret of Mirror Bay	448-09549-1
☐ 21 The Secret in the Old Attic	448-09521-1	☐ 50 The Double Jinx Mystery	448-09550-5
☐ 22 Clue in the Crumbling Wall	448-09522-X	☐ 51 Mystery of the Glowing Eye	448-09551-3
☐ 23 Mystery of the Tolling Bell	448-09523-8	☐ 52 The Secret of the Forgotten City	448-09552-1
☐ 24 Clue in the Old Album	448-09524-6	☐ 53 The Sky Phantom	448-09553-X
☐ 25 Ghost of Blackwood Hall	448-09525-4	☐ 54 The Strange Message in the Parchment	448-09554-8
☐ 26 Clue of the Leaning Chimney	448-09526-2	☐ 55 Mystery of Crocodile Island	448-09555-6
☐ 27 Secret of the Wooden Lady	448-09527-0	☐ 56 The Thirteenth Pearl	448-09556-4
☐ 28 The Clue of the Black Keys	448-09528-9		
☐ 29 Mystery at the Ski Jump	448-09529-7		

**VISIT PUTNAM BERKLEY ONLINE
ON THE INTERNET: http://www.putnam.com/berkley**

Payable in U.S. funds. No cash accepted. Postage & handling: $3.50 for one book. $1.00 for each additional. Maximum postage $8.50. Prices, postage and handling charges may change without notice. Visa, Amex, MasterCard call 1-800-788-6262, ext. 1, or fax 1-201-933-2316.

Or, check above books
and send this order form to:

**The Putnam Publishing Group
P.O. Box 12289, Dept. B
Newark, NJ 07101-5289**

Please allow 4-6 weeks for delivery.
Foreign and Canadian delivery 8-12 weeks

Book Total $ _____

Applicable Sales Tax $ _____
(CA, NJ, NY, GST Can.)

Postage & Handling $ _____

Total Amount Due $ _____

Nancy Drew® and The Hardy Boys® are trademarks
of Simon & Schuster, Inc. and are registered
in the United States Patent and Trademark Office.

Bill my: ☐ Visa ☐ MasterCard ☐ Amex _____ (expires)

Card#_____
($10 minimum)

Daytime Phone # _____

Signature_____

Or enclosed is my: ☐ check ☐ money order
SHIP TO:
Name _____
Address _____
City _____ State _____ Zip _____

BILL TO:
Name _____
Address _____
City _____ State _____ Zip _____